Palette of Love

To a great friend, Philosopher and guide and above all a great Boss - BILL

Ashok Kallarakkal

Another engrossing collection of Short Stories
From the Author of

Curiosity Kills the KatHA

FROG BOOKS

First published in India 2013 by Frog Books
An imprint of Leadstart Publishing Pvt Ltd
1 Level, Trade Centre
Bandra Kurla Complex
Bandra (East) Mumbai 400 051 India
Telephone: +91-22-40700804
Fax: +91-22-40700800
Email: info@leadstartcorp.com
www.leadstartcorp.com / www.frogbooks.net

Sales Office:
Unit No.25/26, Building No.A/1,
Near Wadala RTO,
Wadala (East), Mumbai – 400037 India
Phone: +91 22 24046887

US Office:
Axis Corp, 7845 E Oakbrook Circle
Madison, WI 53717 USA

ISBN 978-93-83562-15-2

Book Editor: Rajan Bhatia
Design Editor: Mishta Roy
Layout: Chandravadan R. Shiroorkar

Typeset in Book Antiqua
Printed at Repro India Ltd, Mumbai

Price — India: Rs 125; Elsewhere: US $5

About the Author

Ashok Kallarakkal (Dr. T K Ashok Kumar) is a senior Management/IT professional working out of Bangalore. He is an engineering graduate from REC Calicut (now NIT Calicut) and did his doctorate in International Business from Indian Institute of Management (IIM) Bangalore.

Ashok's first book, a collection of short stories 'Curiosity Kills the KatHA' was published in August 2012 by Leadstart Publishers, Mumbai. It has received rave reviews from readers and the media alike and is available worldwide.

Ashok had written a number of science fiction stories in popular regional science magazines like Shastra Keralam in his school days, but had curtailed his urge to write more, to devote time for higher education and building a career like every other middle class youth.

He rediscovered his flair for writing fiction while writing innumerable sales proposals as part of his job. His dream now is to spend more and more time on creative writing and other passions (Though this does not mean moving back to a sales job).

Ashok teaches management students at various institutes, conducts corporate trainings on various subjects ranging from product management to creativity and innovation. He is a Master Neuro-Linguistic Programming trainer and provides coaching and mentoring to upcoming leaders in the industry.

Ashok, now, is working on his first novel.

He is a MENSA member and his wife Sandhya, is a lawyer turned software professional turned homemaker. Their only child Anjali is a third grade student and is a regular character along with her mother in many of his stories.

You can reach Ashok on e-mail at ashoktk@gmail.com.

Important Links:

https://www.facebook.com/PaletteOfLove2013

www.facebook.com/ashokkallarakkal

www.amazon.com/author/ashok

www.facebook.com/Curiositykillsthekatha

Dedication

To my parents who initiated me into the world of letters, encouraged me to think independently, taught me to voice my opinions politely without fear, and above all spent their lifetime toiling to make me what I am today.

Acknowledgements

It is difficult to thank all who contributed to making this book a reality because that would call for an entire book by itself. Here, I would like to mention a few who come to my mind:

First of all, I would like to thank my dear wife Sandhya, the perfect project manager and task master, for doing more than just encouraging me to write this book. She would closely monitor my daily outputs and had secretly made a PERT chart to monitor my writing, to ensure there is always a float. Till this day, she refuses to share this plan with me, though admitting that she had such a plan!

She and Anjali (our only daughter) need to be also thanked for creating occasions (inadvertently) which sowed the seeds for some of the stories, and agreeing to be characters in them. Anjali is also probably my only fan as a writer though she has not successfully finished reading even one of my stories.

A special thank you to Nalinakumari – my mother-in- law, for reading my stories and responding to them objectively and critically thus giving me confidence.

Many thanks to Radhika Nathan, my ex-colleague at IBM, whose debutant novel 'Mute Anklet' is expected to hit the stands soon, for reviewing the stories and giving me critical comments. Many thanks to Shevlin Sebastian (Sr. Reporter, The New Indian Express), Chris (Feature Reporter, Deccan Chronicle), M.K. Harikumar (Literary Critic), Sudhakaraan Chanthavila (Poet and Critic), Sunil Kumar (Reporter, Mathrubhumi) and Morgen Bailey (Writer and Critic) for reviewing my first book 'Curiosity Kills the KatHA' . I learnt a lot from their critical comments. Thanks to their critical reviews, the book was a success.

I would like to thank Rajan Bhatia and Mishta Roy – my editor and cover designer respectively, for converting this collection into a covetable book.

A big thank you to Swarup Nanda, and his company Leadstart Publishing, for reposing faith in me again, and agreeing to publish my second book.

Above all, I thank the omnipotent force, which drives the universe – call it God or Nature, for endowing me with all that it takes to write a book like this.

Contents

All for the Girl

'Come fast,' I shouted.

I was waiting near the Lalbagh[1] parking lot for the last two hours and at half past one, my stomach was rumbling loudly.

The tourist bus, with 'Government Law College, Cochin' banner hoisted in the front, which started its journey from Cochin, had taken unusually long time to reach the garden city.

My wait was particularly excruciating because I had skipped work for the day without informing anyone.

Sandhya slowly appeared from the bus carrying a small handbag, which looked more like an oversized purse.

'That is all you have?' I asked a bit surprised.

'My God, am I going to marry into a poor family?' I added.

'Don't you worry Ashok . . . she has another big bag which we were supposed to take to the hotel room. We can give it to you, but your scrawny motorcycle won't suffice' - one of her friends attempted a dig at me.

'Look at the guy's cheek. Is he marrying for money?' someone chirped in.

---

[1] A sprawling green park in Bangalore.

'Oh my sweet sisters, that was an attempted joke. *Matrimony is a Matter of money* - someone had once said', I tried to escape the sharp tongues of a dozen emerging woman lawyers.

'Ashokji, it is now one thirty. We do not care that you guys are getting married in a couple of months. You have to return our sweet friend to the hotel room, by nine p.m. Otherwise, we would send a police force after you to conduct your marriage in Bangalore itself' - one of the students with an American accent instructed me.

'Your wish is my command ma'am' I feigned obedience.

'You will not get to see them, till we start back from Bangalore,' said another one.

I did not wait to listen to the catcalls and the less palatable remarks emanating from the back seats, where the boys were preparing to get down. I started my Yamaha motorcycle and signaled Sandhya to jump in.

She climbed the backseat with great difficulty, thanks to her five feet frame. I was amused at her predicament but dared not laugh. We left the parking lot in a hurry.

I don't want to be harassed anymore in front of my fiancée, I thought

Our marriage was fixed three months back. It was, like most marriages in our part of the world, an 'arranged one'. She was the second girl I met and mutually evaluated, in the presence of parents and elders from either side. The first one had politely turned me down. It was a short meeting. In less than fifteen minutes, all of them unanimously decided that we were made for each other. Some of the more spiritually inclined even went on to claim that God had already carved our names together in stone. We were destined to be married to each other.

Like all 'well brought up kids, both of us accepted and agreed with their wishes. I, a well-paid management professional, working for a multinational company in the software industry, did not find anything wrong with her. Neither did she, a final year law student, find anything unacceptable about me.

The compatibility and parity in religion, caste, creed, class, color, and *matching kundalis* (astrological signs) made it a perfect match, even from an ill-wisher's perspective.

The engagement took place two weeks later in my absence, as is normal in Kerala. We had been engaged for the last three months. The marriage was scheduled to be held a week after her final exams.

I, working in Bangalore, and she, studying in Cochin, never got opportunities to meet after the life changing ten minutes we had spent together to make the decision.

My desperate phone calls to her usually had an uncanny way of being attended by her father, who firmly believed that unmarried girls should never talk to men, even to their grooms-to-be!

That is when the lord almighty smiled on us in the form of an excursion from her law college. Now she is sitting behind me on my motorcycle. This was our first date and we have a few precious hours to spend together, all by ourselves.

'Let us have lunch first. I am famished ' I said, as soon as we crossed the main gate.

Silence!

'What would you like to have? Veg or non-veg, lunch, or should we have sandwiches, may be a pizza, your choice.' I tried hard to get some response from her through my multiple-choice question.

Silence again!

I remembered what one of my married friends once said, 'You get to talk only till you get married.'

'Hey Sandhyaji, are you still there?'

I could only hear her instant giggle.

'OK, here we go.' I turned the throttle and with a deafening roar, we picked up speed. We crossed 80 kph in no time.

A good start to impress her.

I weaved in and out of the traffic like a man possessed.

'Drive slowly please,' I got a tug on my back with a reasonably loud request.

Having accomplished my mission, I slowed down. 'So you talk too. I had forgotten to test that when we met last time. I almost thought you were dumb.'

Giggle again!

'Here we are. Welcome to McDonalds!' I said as I stopped the bike in front of their new outlet at Hosur Road.

'What would you have?' I asked again, this time looking straight into her eyes, having seated comfortably opposite her at a corner table.

'Whatever you like,' she said with a charming diffidence.

I walked to the counter and picked up two McChicken meals.

'You had sandwiches before?' I wanted to rub in the fact that she was from a rural suburb in Kerala while I had the luck to be educated and be based in a cosmopolitan city like Bangalore.

'This is not sandwich Ashok, this is burger' she not only corrected me but my pre-conceived notions as well.

'How are my would be parents-in-law? 'I tried to cover it up by asking a mundane question.

'Happy till I left them,' she answered.

Did she intend a pun there? I was a bit skeptical about her responses.

'Where do you want to go next? Or is that also left to me?' I decided to take the offensive on to a different track.

'Left to yourself, where would you take me next?' – A counter question, just like a lawyer.

'Let me see...may be for a movie,' I said.

'Not a bad idea, if not a movie, what other options would you consider?' She was gaining confidence by the second.

'A mall or say a good book shop?'

Before she could comment, I had a *Eureka* moment.

'Why not a park? We can probably go to Cubbon Park; [2]you do not have such parks in Kerala.'

'You *dumbo,* we just came out of Lalbagh gardens and you want to go to another park? I thought my parents had found me an intelligent guy,' she laughed and got on the offensive.

I felt deflated but happy. I wanted such a playful partner for life, not the mushy traditional type.

'Oh OK, I give up. Your Excellency, please tell me where you want to be driven to?' I feigned anger and resignation.

'Will you take me, if I tell you?' She suddenly sounded like a child.

'Definitely, even if it is to hell, as long as you are with me,' I tried some filmy dialogue.

---

[2] Another big park in the middle of Bangalore.

'No, don't say hell and all' she said seriously and closed my mouth with her palms.

'You didn't tell me where,' I was getting restless.

'I will tell you. But promise me you would take me wherever it is,' the child came back again.

'Granted,' I said firmly.

'I want to buy a nice Ganesha[3] idol, she said slowly, studying my reaction to every word.

'Is that all? Let us go to *Cauvery Handicrafts* on M.G. Road,' I got up.

'Not there,' she said.

I sat back as if pulled down.

'I want a stone idol'

'*Cauvery* has stone ones too'

'No, I was told that, near Hosur - on the Tamil Nadu side - artisans sit by the road and sculpt statues. I want to see that and buy an idol from there,' she elaborated on what she wanted.

I suddenly realized why every guy I had met in the past had been so scared about his girl's shopping preferences.

'It will be a long ride,' I tried to dissuade her.

She realized my reluctance.

'We have time, need to reach back only by nine' she thwarted my attempt.

'We would end up spending all the time we got, on this goddamn bike,' my favorite motorcycle suddenly lost my affection and received a treatment normally reserved for villains.

---

[3] A Hindu God with an Elephant face.

Anyway, we have a long time for spending on other things,' she said with a devilish smile.

I realized I would look silly if I try anymore to avoid the trip.

Henceforth, you decide and I will execute - I thought in subjugation.

'If you don't want to go, it is fine with me,' the smile was still there.

Penultimate weapon in the bag! Second only to crying! - She knew I could never say 'no' to that.

Never think 'never'. Not now, I will learn to say 'no' after the marriage.

'Let us go' I said sounding enthusiastic, without directly responding to her taunt.

I realized what non-stop transmission, claimed by 24/7 radio stations, is as I drove down National Highway 7 towards Hosur. Sandhya was continuously transmitting information and I was intermittently receiving them. Soon, I realized the futility of trying to understand the complex network of relationships her family had and the unique likes, dislikes, interests, characteristics, attitudes etc. of each node in the network.

As she had already said, we have a lot of time ahead for all that.

When you drive with a helmet covering your ears, and a gushing wind against your face, you can never hear what your pillion is trying to say, especially so, if the speaker is your fiancée or wife, who you would not mind avoiding, as against a girl friend. In this case, I was sure she cared less about me really understanding the chatter.

It took nearly one and a half hours to cross the Karnataka border to Tamil Nadu. The Bangalore winter made the journey a bit easier than normal, though the continuous traffic jams remained unnerving.

I was unhappy about not being able to spend some quality time with my bride to be. I would rather have sat in a park or a coffee shop and discussed the proverbial *sweet nothings* instead.

It took another twenty minutes before we found the first shop selling stone statues. It was a tent where two-three artisans sat around and worked while their wives shouted at each other loudly and their children ran around falling down often.

Gods sat around and smiled!

As soon I got down, I saw a seven feet statue of Ganesha, which could have easily weighed a few hundred kilos. I ran to it and shouted -

'Sandy . . . here it is, the perfect one for your house.' I have this unique capability to make even innocuous comments sound sarcastic.

'If only a millionaire was marrying me, I would have built a house which could hold that statue, unlucky me,' she retorted in jest with a sad face.

I accepted defeat.

'OK, you select. Let me understand your tastes.'

She went inside the tent and started looking around. I, like a chastened child, followed her.

She kept looking at each statue with lot of interest in the beginning and after few minutes of intense study, moved on to the next one. I realized that the exercise could take hours.

'Hey, I like this one' I picked up a small Ganesha, about one foot tall, without particularly liking it. I just wanted her to make up her mind quickly, be done with the purchase, so that she could spend time with me, her future husband.

'Ashok, what did you see in that? Look at the sharp edges of the trunk, the trunk is also bent awkwardly. It is bad,' she derided my selection.

'Madam is right sir. That is a bad piece. You do not want to buy that' the shabbily dressed attendant standing at the corner of the store seconded her opinion.

I tried to hide my face behind some statues, - at least figuratively. How I wished I knew more about sculptures and art. I could have impressed Sandhya, with my knowledge!

I started seriously looking at the options. I was not interested in selecting the statue quickly. I wanted to select the best option so that I could really impress her, regaining my lost esteem.

After examining a dozen idols thrown on the floor in the makeshift store room, which formed a major part of the tent, braving unidentified running kids, I found a piece which was devoid of any of the defects, Sandhya had mentioned earlier. It looked good, almost perfect.

Deciding to make the most of my luck in finding the apparently ideal piece, I called out to her hunched over a set of smaller idols, at the other end of the tent 'Sandy, here is the one you want.'

Hearing the excitement in my voice, she kept back the piece she was holding in her right hand and came running towards me, closely followed by the attendant.

She took the idol in her hand, examined it critically, and nodded approvingly.

I was elated. I acted as if the whole selection process was a piece of cake for me.

Then her eyes narrowed, critically examining the idol again. She looked shocked and put the idol back on the floor.

'This won't work,' she said as she moved to examine other idols.

'Why?' I asked frustrated at having been once again let down.

'The trunk is towards the right side.'

I examined Ganesha's trunk critically and noticed it was curving towards the right.

'So what, Ganesha has to keep it somewhere, either to the left or to the right. Look here, this one is to the left, and that one is curved to the right.'

I was wounded more by the condescending smile, which appeared on the attendant's face.

What is this guy laughing about?

'Ashok, you don't know this!' Sandhya started at me not knowing how to handle an ignorant, dumb fool like me. 'Ganesha, with trunk towards the right side, is seldom kept at home. Because it demands strict ritualistic care. He is very demanding. We should only buy one with a trunk curving to the left,' she explained as if she was educating an idiot.

Of course, I did not know that and I did not know a million other things as well. So what? She is stuck with me, this stupid fellow, I thought.

'Madam is right sir,' the attendant tried to rub it in.

I decided not to show my ignorance anymore. What worried me more was that she had not even noticed my silence and lack of cooperation in the buying process for the next two hours.

Shopping is the opium of the lasses- my chauvinistic mind concluded.

Three more tents and two hours later, we found the ideal idol! She was happy and I felt that it was a worthwhile ordeal. At least, I helped in finding whatever she wanted.

'Ashok, thanks a lot for being so patient. My dad would have disowned me if I took so much time shopping,' she told as we got back to the bike.

I too would have, If I had an option, I wanted to say.

'I will hold the idol' Sandhya said, once again climbing the bike with great difficulty.

As the friendly attendant in the tent handed over the Ganesha neatly packed in an old newspaper, we both realized that it would be extremely uncomfortable for Sandhya to sit in the pillion holding on my shoulders while keeping it on her lap.

The clever man did not take much time to propose and implement a difficult though workable solution.

Thus the idol, weighing over three kilograms, wrapped in three strong polythene bags and hung on the handle bar of my motorcycle danced to each gutter and stone on the road as we rode back in the dark.

Sandhya re-started the incessant babble. I sincerely prayed that she would not ask any question on the subjects covered, on reaching our destination. *I could not afford to fail another test.*

The ride was comfortable, but I tried some rash techniques to impress her. My score on that front so far had been negative anyway. I was a loser, unable to impress her.

I was promptly chided and I realized she has already usurped the 'wife' role and I am done for life.

But to my surprise, I loved her even more for just that. I took a turn at the Ring Road and turned again and now we were travelling on the interior roads.

'Where are you taking me?' my pillion rider asked. I could sense some concern in her voice.

'Are you scared to come with me, wherever it is?' I asked jokingly.

For the first time she seemed to have lost the battle. She did not respond.

'Hey, I was joking. I am taking you directly to your hotel. This is a short cut and we can reach the hotel faster.

'I thought you would buy me dinner before taking me to the hotel. That is why I asked... You *kanjoos*[4]' she tried to regain her lost ground.

'Liar-Lawyer' I said rhyming the words.

She laughed as we continued down the empty lanes.

I did not see him at all.

Sandhya shouted in my ears a bit too late and anyway I could not have heard her with my helmet on.

By the time I saw him, emerging from the shadows, it was too late. The road was blocked with couple of stones and some wooden pieces.

I stopped the bike. The guy, in his late thirties, disheveled and wearing soiled clothes, pushed a long knife under my jaw and signaled me to get down.

---

[4] Kanjoos - 'Miser' in Hindi.

I did and so did Sandhya.

I was scared, more for her than for myself.

'Give me all your money, and I will spare your life,' the guy demanded in Hindi, waving the knife in the air.

I pulled out my purse and tried to extract money from it. Then looking at his face, I realized, it was more prudent to hand over the purse itself to him.

I did.

With faltering fingers, he examined the purse, and extracted all the money from it and returned it to me.

'You have only this much?' He asked in a threatening tone. Desperation was written all over his face.

'I don't have any more money,' I said, as a matter of fact.

'This is not enough' he said

He kept the knife closer to my throat and turned his attention to Sandhya.

'How much money you have? Out with everything' he commanded.

Sandhya was in tears. She quickly opened her handbag and pulled out all the money she had in it.

I prayed for a miracle, like a police jeep coming on the same road. However, no such miracle happened. The guy had picked up the right spot.

He quickly counted the money.

'Not enough.' His knife kept drawing random shapes in the air.

Sandhya started removing her necklace and earrings. She was sobbing.

My knees started weakening.

The ultimate failure of a guy - failing to provide security to his girl even on the first date! I hung my head in shame.

The guy started rummaging through my backpack.

Sandhya started praying under her breath. I could hear her saying 'Namah Shivaya' repeatedly.

Not finding anything valuable, the robber snatched Sandhya's handbag and turned his attention to its contents.

He could not find anything valuable.

He moved the knife from my throat to Sandhya's throat.

'There is an ATM round the corner. Get me twenty five thousand from the ATM immediately. If you try anything funny, I will kill her.' he said, looking menacing.

He took my wallet again and gave me the ATM card.

I could not leave her with this guy and go, so I did not move.

He grew wild and more desperate. He pressed the knife harder on Sandhya's throat.

She screamed in pain.

I could not stand it anymore. On the one hand my would-be-bride was being treated badly in front of me, and on the other, I was rendered helpless to react when I desperately had to regain my already lost esteem, in front of her.

In courtship, reason sometimes deserts you. It was one of those moments, a moment of desperation.

Without thinking about the outcome, I picked up the plastic bag and swung it in a lightning move.

One last-ditch attempt to regain my prestige, to prove my manliness, to save my girl.

A single block of stone weighing more than three kilos made an arc in the air at a terrific speed and made contact with a comparatively soft skull bringing down the person instantly.

His body twitched once and lay still. Blood started oozing out making designs on the road.

I did not check whether Sandhya was impressed; I knew she would be.

We jumped on the bike and I raced ahead like a mad man. The helmet had fallen of somewhere, and the chilling breeze failed to cool me.

I did not even notice that Sandhya had managed to jump on to the bike, with consummate ease this time, even with the Ganesha idol held close to her heart like an infant.

I felt happy that I could prove my manliness at the right moment. *That was a God given opportunity!*

'Was he dead?' she asked.

I applied sudden break as the enormity of what I had done dawned on me.

'I don't know. Let us hope he is not,' I said.

'Let us do something. We need to save him if he is still alive,' she suggested.

I dialed an emergency number and informed the police about a certain body we had seen on the road while passing by.

In a few minutes, we hit the main road.

'Let us have some coffee. I cannot stand the pressure' she suggested.

We stopped at one of the coffee shop chains, made ourselves comfortable in one corner, and ordered two lattes.

'I do not have any money on me. My purse was in that guy's hand' I said.

'My purse is empty. You saw that,' Sandhya added.

'How will we pay for the coffee?' my thoughts came out loud.

'Don't you worry about that. My mobile always has some extra currency.'

'Mobile currency to pay the restaurant bill? I am not in a mood for jokes.' My voice was harsh.

'I was not joking.' She opened the back of her mobile phone and pulled out the battery. There, to my surprise and relief, was a well-concealed five hundred rupee note.

'Thank God,' I said.

She tried to smile. But her fingers still shivered a bit due to fear.

'Do not worry. Everything would be fine'; I tried to pacify her.' I got scared. I thought he would kill us if he could not find enough money,' her voice was trembling.

'I knew, with just one attacker, I could spring a surprise. It is all about waiting for the right moment,' I tried to act macho.

I could see a faint admiration in her eyes. *She approves her man!*

We tried to talk about other things to bring ourselves back to normalcy, but conversation always clawed back to the incident quickly.

My phone rang.

'This is Sub Inspector Murugesh. Are you Mr. Ashok?' a gruff voice from the other side spoke.

'Yes sir,' I tried to bring as much calmness too my voice as possible, while my heart was beating as if there is no tomorrow.

'We found your purse on a man brought in bad condition to St. Johns. Can you come over to the hospital and identify the purse? I also need to talk to you.'

'Sure sir, I will be there in fifteen minutes,' I said and disconnected the phone.

'Sandhya, I will get you an auto to go back to the hotel. I need to go to the hospital. Remember,- for all practical purposes, you were not with me when the incident occurred, 'I said as we walked out.

'No, I am coming with you, wherever it is. Moreover, it makes sense to keep me in the picture. Hitting a person, attacking a woman with a knife will get pardoned more easily,' she argued liked a trained lawyer.

'Moreover, we are together in everything Ashok,' she said pressing my palm reassuringly.

'I was waiting for you.' Inspector Murugesh greeted us, at St. John's hospital.

'Here is the purse ... it is yours ... right?' he asked.

'Yes, that is mine' I acted out the happiness of a person who just found his lost purse.

'And I am sure you have an explanation too.' The police officer's tone was not very reassuring.

'Of course, while returning from Hosur, we saw this guy lying on the road. I stopped my bike and squatted down near him to check. It must have fallen off from my back pocket. I was the one who called the emergency number.'

'I thought so. I had already checked the numbers and they match. You do one thing. You take your cards etc. and leave just the purse with me. I will keep that for investigation. If other things go to the station, you may never see them again.' He laughed at his own joke.

I was not in a mood to laugh; neither was Sandhya.

'Sir, how is the guy?' I summoned courage and asked.

'Not dead yet. Unless they operate on him immediately, he won't survive. His skull is broken and there are blood clots in the brain.'

'Sir, did he say how this happened,' I pushed my luck a bit.

'You can go inside and see him. But be careful and, don't make noise in the casualty ward.' He walked to his Jeep without answering my question.

Sandhya and I looked at each other. We went inside the Casualty ward. Most beds were empty.

Then I saw the guy with bandages all over his head. A sleepy policeman stood a bit far away from him, watching what was happening around with total disinterest.

'Murugesh sir sent you? It was your purse, wasn't it? he asked as we walked closer to the bed.

The figure on the bed saw us and signaled us to come closer.

The man had lost his fury; but the desperation was still there.

With a little difficulty, he started talking in a slow, hushed tone.

'I am sorry,' he said.

We were surprised.

'We got you into this state!' I said.

'I have only a few hours to live. They can save me if they operate on my skull in the next couple of hours. It will cost fifty thousand. I don't have that kind of money. So, I am bound to die. I do not have any regret about that. I deserve to die probably for trying to stop you on the way and demanding money at knife point.'

Though he summarized his status without allowing us to say anything, difficulty in talking was quite evident.

I did not know what to say. Sandhya also looked confused.

'Forget all that. I need help from you. This is a request. You need to give me thirty thousand rupees,' he begged.

'You said you need fifty for your surgery?' I interjected.

'That money is not for me. I will tell you. Remember the big earthquake in Gujarat last year. The one, which killed over twenty thousand people? I was one of the unfortunates who lost everything in that disaster. But, fate had spared my wife and me, as on that day, we had gone to another village for a festival. Reduced to absolute poverty, we came south searching for work. That is how I became a laborer at one of the construction sites in Yelehanka. '

I was in no mood to listen to stories at this late hour. I wanted to escape, but the fear of being named as a murderer made me stay put and see if I could negotiate a way out with this guy.

I also did not want my girl to think that I was heartless.

'My wife delivered a baby girl in the government hospital three days back. Initially everything was fine. Soon, our daughter started breathing heavily, indicating some abnormalities. She was born with a severe heart disease. Doctors called it CHD[5] or something like that. We brought her to this hospital, this morning for a critical surgery. She is in neonatal ward, bed number four.'

He paused as his breathing became a bit labored.

'I needed thirty thousand for her operation. We did not have any money. We did not even know anyone here. There is no relative back in Gujarat who could help us. I tried selling my kidney through a tout this afternoon. Police caught me and warned me. Out of options, I decided to find an isolated road and rob someone.'

'God failed me even in that,' he started crying.

I did not know what to say.

'Will you please give me thirty thousand to save my daughter? This is a dying man's request,' he pleaded.

'Silence please,' a nurse shouted from a corner desk.

'I will do one thing in return. I have not given any statement to the police yet. If you pay me the money, I will lie to police in my *dying declaration*[6]. I will say a truck hit me.'

'You are blackmailing me? How dare you do that?' I asked with my voice raised in anger and frustration.

Sandhya tapped me, signaling to calm down.

'I am desperate. I will do anything to save my daughter. I was ready to sell my kidneys. I ambushed you for money. Now I

---

[5] CHD - Congenital Heart Defect, one of the most common birth defects. One of the symptoms often is the shortness of breath.

[6] Dying Declaration has a lot of value in India based on the principle a man will not meet his Maker with a lie in his mouth.

am dying in my effort to save her. Don't you see I would do anything to save *my girl*, including blackmail.'

I did not say anything.

'They will come for the *dying declaration* any moment. You decide if thirty thousand is too much for your freedom and my daughter's life.'

I was ready to pay the amount for my absolution. But what if, he takes the money and then names me as the culprit?

'Let me think,' I said and walked towards the door, closely followed by Sandhya.

As I passed the lone police man, he whispered in my ears, 'Sir, he is lying.'

'What?' I exclaimed.

'He is lying. You don't pay any money. He has already given the *dying declaration* stating that a truck had hit him. I heard your conversation. You don't need to pay him anything,' the policeman explained.

'I looked back at the man lying motionless on the bed. His face continued to plead, but had the smile of a boy caught stealing chocolates.

'Are you the person, who came with this patient?' A nurse came towards us in a hurry and enquired.

I did not say anything.

'You need to deposit fifty thousand rupees at the counter. If we do not operate in an hour, he won't survive.'

She thrust a piece of paper displaying the ICU bed number with a figure of fifty thousand against it and continued in the same pace as she came in.

'Fifty thousand for this and thirty thousand for the baby girl at neonatal ward, bed number four,' I said firmly, as I pushed my credit card and the paper given to me by the nurse, through the counter.

Sandhya looked at me with mixed emotions.

This time, I was not seeking admiration and was not interested in impressing anyone, not even my girl!

****

Winter Rain

'Rohit Shenoy became the *destroyer* through hard work and dedication. There was a time when the second child of a laborer family in a little known village in Kanakapura went without food for days, but walked all the way to the Karnataka State Cricket Association stadium on M.G. road to watch his idols Sunil Gavaskar and Sandeep Patil play.'

The television anchor holding the wireless microphone was at ease, continuing the endless introduction in front of the camera. After all, it was not a live telecast; someone was going to edit and prune it. Secondly, there was nothing wrong in showing off the arduous preparation she had done for this program.

I am going to hit big time with this interview, she kept telling herself.

The camera was focused on her with the palatial bungalow of the great cricketer in the background. As an evening shot, sun setting behind the camera lent a golden glow to the tastefully architected building.

'Such a shot would encourage every kid to take up cricket as their path to riches' her producer had told her.

Path of cricket to riches! What a rip-off? she thought.

Of a couple of hundred thousand kids who take up cricket every ten years, at the most thirty or forty would make it big. Rest of them would have squandered opportunities for education and sustainable jobs wasting their adolescence on the game! she calculated.

'Come... let us go and talk to Rohit the *destroyer* about his preparations for the new test series starting tomorrow with the world number one Australia. This would be all the more interesting as the first test he would be playing after his recent marriage . . . ' with this, she turned and started running towards the main door with the camera following her.

After a few steps, the cameraman switched off the camera and the powerful flashlights. The next shot will be taken when the anchor knocks at the door. Rohit would then open the door and welcome them acting quite surprised about the TV crew visiting his house. This scene was discussed and rehearsed many times.

Unfortunately, the ace player's deadpan face fails to register any emotion most times, the cameraman mused. Probably, that is what makes him a feared opponent.

Finally, they were inside the house. The production team had already arranged the house furniture in the courtyard in such a way that they could position three cameras without any one of them, even accidentally, coming in others' focus.

The anchor, dressed in black T-shirt and light blue jeans, was wearing flat-heeled shoes, for a change, as she did not want to look taller than Rohit. He, at Five Feet Four inches, needs to look much taller during the interview.

'Whoever had named Rohit, did name him right. The anchor thought. '"Raw - Hit" did explain his playing style'

'Rohit, thanks a lot for agreeing to spend time with the millions of viewers of *"Suvarna Chitra"* channel, especially on the eve of such a long awaited match'.' She made the opening remark for the hour-long interview, scheduled to be aired as part of the run up to the match, later in the evening.

'It is my pleasure. What I am today is made possible by the prayers and love of each one of you.' Rohit responded looking directly at the camera acting as if he is addressing the millions of viewers directly.

Poor guy! His face does not show the humility he is trying to portray, thought the main cameraman. Frequent interactions, as part of the television crew, had taught him that Rohit, notwithstanding his wooden face, was actually a nice human being.

One of the very few, who has not been affected by fame and money! he thought.

'So Rohit, how do you see the challenges likely to be posed by the new crop of Australian quickies?'

Clad in a crystal clean white *kurta* and pajama, Rohit looked more like a politician on the eve of polling rather than a successful cricketer.

'Did you mean Dave and Bob?' Rohit asked.

Rohit knew very well, that the anchor was referring to Dave McCurdy and Robert Dilley. But he wanted to buy time before answering.

Time to think up the most politically correct answer.

'Bob is a great bowler. He has proved his worth quite well in the last few months, especially in fast tracks of England and Jamaica. But I am sure...'

He was interrupted half way, by an anxious face at the door opposite to him. The anchor could not see it and neither could the cameras.

The door opened to his office room. He knew that his wife will not signal to him the way she did, unless there was some emergency. Someone important must be waiting for him in the office. Since the room had a door opening directly towards the front garden, he could not have seen the visitor coming in.

Whoever it is, it must be important, he thought.

'Let me come back in a second ... ' Rohit got up in a hurry and walked briskly towards the door.

'The guy's name is Shivanna. He wants to meet you and says it is critical. He almost forced his way in. Is this the same Shivanna you had talked to me about, a few times? He seems to be in bad shape,' his wife Kavitha whispered in his ears.

Rohit entered the room and closed the door behind.

'Shivanna! What is happening to you?' he asked the figure sprawled on the sofa.

Kavitha sighed. She did not like the way the uninvited guest had barged in and the way he was making himself comfortable on her sofa.

Shivanna did not answer.

Rohit went and sat near Shivanna on the sofa. He could see that Shivanna was drunk.

He was dressed in a long sleeves slack shirt and tight black trousers. The expensive clothes advertised his brand loyalties loudly. His shoes and socks were strewn on the floor in his hurry to make the sofa his temporary bed.

Kavitha did not like the fact that he had not removed his leather shoes, no matter how expensive they were, before entering the room.

She never allowed footwear inside the house.

In fact, Rohit always talked about an imaginary dust-repellant-walking-shoe, which he wanted to champion with an ad showing Kavitha allowing it inside the house without thinking twice.

'Shivanna, please, what is this all about? Look at you, did a liquor tanker run over you?' Rohit asked with concern as he took Shivanna's left hand in his palms.

Shivanna sat up on the sofa. He was unable to balance himself and sit straight. His face showed beads of sweat despite it being a December evening in Bangalore.

He folded both hands together. Rohit could imagine what was being asked silently. They never needed words or even a language to talk to each other. They could communicate without words, with an uncanny ability to read each other's thoughts.

Shivanna needed help! This was the first time Shivanna was asking something from him!

'Rohit...you need to help me.'

Before Rohit could ask anything more, his mobile rang.

'Oh, I am sorry . . . I will be there in a moment,' Rohit answered the television Anchor who reminded him that time was running out for their interview. The interview had to go on air in couple of hours.

'Shivanna, you relax. Whatever it is, we will discuss it after I come back. I will just finish this interview in half an hour or so and be back'.

Shivanna did not respond. He looked ill at ease.

'Shivanna, I need to go...Do not worry. Kavitha will take good care of you,' he said as he walked out without waiting for Shivanna's response.

'Kavitha, do not go anywhere. I want you to be with Shivanna. You ask Jayamma to get him some buttermilk or sour curd,' he instructed Kavitha and made sure Shivanna too heard it.

'Kavitha, be here with him, do not allow him to go anywhere or do anything rash,' he whispered as he passed Kavitha who was still standing near the door.

Rohit walked out and closed the door behind him. He did not want the TV crew to notice what was going on inside.

Kavitha looked at Shivanna. He seemed to be in his late fifties. His face, though tired, still showed evidences of aristocracy and riches.

'Shivanna, can I help you with something?' Kavitha moved closer to the sofa and asked.

'Let me get you some curd. It would help you combat the spirits...' she said as if she had years of experience with drunkards.

In her home, nobody drank. In fact, drinks were strictly forbidden at her home. But she had read enough to have a basic idea as to why Rohit prescribed buttermilk or sour curd.

Instead of calling Jayamma the maid, she herself went to the kitchen and got some really sour curd from the refrigerator.

She did not want Jayamma to notice a drunkard in her room.

Shivanna emptied the tumbler as if he had been thirsty for a long time.

'Shivanna, why don't you wash your face and freshen up a bit?' Kavitha said.

'Oh dear, I am sorry I look like this, not the right way to meet you for the first time. But let me tell you Rohit is lucky; you are definitely the ideal wife for him. I can see kindness in your eyes,' Shivanna said as he walked to the bathroom.

From the time he came in, Kavitha had developed a growing dislike for him. But she had heard that Shivanna had played an important role in Rohit's life. That was the only reason; she humored the man, despite him being drunk.

But she felt a slight change in her disposition on hearing Shivanna's words; she wanted to fight it hard for she did not like the tinge of indebtedness in Rohit's actions, on meeting the man.

She was possessive about her husband, just like any other newlywed.

Shivanna returned in a much better state. He looked much more presentable, though his eyes remained blood shot.

He took a cigarette from his pocket and kept it on his lips.

Kavitha wanted to stop him. She did not like people smoking indoors; it always left a stink.

But she did not venture to.

Shivanna sat with the cigarette jutting from his mouth, focused on some imaginary scene at a far off place. Then he pulled out the cigarette and threw it in the dustbin.

Kavitha let off another sigh, this time, of relief, and that too silently.

'I do not smoke nowadays, kicked the habit a year back' he said.

'But you were about to . . . ' Kavitha did not believe him.

'I was a chain smoker for a long time. Then I had acute bronchitis... severe problem in the lungs,' Shivanna said touching his chest.

Kavitha did not say anything. She walked across and sat on a chair directly facing Shivanna.

'Doctors told me not to touch cigarettes. I would not have bothered; a few extra years are not worthwhile, you know, if you cannot enjoy a nice smoke,' he laughed.

Kavitha could feel hollowness in his laugh.

He is talking for the sake of it. His mind is not here, she thought.

'But . . . your man, Rohit, a gem he is. He got me to kick the habit once and for all. It is very difficult to disrespect when someone demands something in the name of love, you know.'

So that is it, she thought. He is here to demand something in the name of love; Something Rohit would not be able to refuse.

'So, nowadays whenever I have an urge to smoke, I put a cigarette between my lips and then look for a lighter which I never carry. Since I cannot light it, I throw it away,' he laughed again.

'But **you** would feel like asking someone for lighter or a matchbox . . . won't you?'

'No, I do not ask for favors to anyone, unless my life depended on it,' he said in a serious tone, as if she had questioned his integrity.

'My friend's grandfather died of lung cancer caused by smoking,' she said to cover up her shock on the retort.

'Poor guy would have coughed and coughed and coughed, till death showed up on his door step. How long had he been bed ridden?'

'Over a year . . .'

'I would never allow that function as a bad example to everyone while you wait for the inevitable death. You know when kids come to visit you, parents would tell, *"look at the old man, he smoked throughout his life and now see, he is suffering a terrible death . . . this is why we say smoking is bad . . . you should always remember his face; then you would never feel like smoking."* Then the kids would look at the old man, laugh and think *"stupid old man. He should have listened to his parents,"* Shivanna stopped as he changed his seating posture.

'I would never allow myself to be made an example like that, an example for the fruits of vices. I would take my life before that,' Shivanna sounded a bit emotional.

Kavitha wondered why he got so excited.

May be he had the onset of lung cancer when he stopped smoking, she thought.

'Rohit and I go a long way. I knew him from his childhood,' Shivanna changed the subject.

This was something of interest to Kavitha. As a newlywed, she never wasted an opportunity to get as much information about her husband, especially about his childhood, his likes etc.

For some reason, she considered those moments to rightfully belong to her though she had missed them altogether.

'You knew him from school days?' she wanted to dig deep.

'Not exactly school days. You know he was born and brought up in a small village on the outskirts called Yedumadu'

'Of course, I know. I have been there. His brother and wife used to stay there till three years back, I guess' she said.

'That is right. After his parents died, his brother brought him up. They had a small hut out there and his brother's family - wife and three children - and Rohit had a hand to mouth existence in Yedumadu.'

Kavitha had met Rohit's brother Rahul and his family several times. It was Rahul and wife Sharada who had first visited her house to see her as part of the marriage proposal process. She knew that Rahul and Sharada were more like parents to Rohit.

'Those days Rahul used to work in a brick making factory and his income was hardly sufficient for their family. That resulted in Rohit dropping out in the seventh standard. But he had two god given gifts - a sharp eye and a lightning reflex,' he stopped for a moment as if to relish his own statement.

'Rohit used to play cricket in the fields with kids from nearby villages. He used to walk and hitch rides to go and watch cricket matches in the city,' he continued.

'I know, television commentators always talk about his walking all the way from his village.'

'Rubbish,' he said 'That is all rubbish. Yedumadu is thirty-two kilometers from the stadium. No one could have walked that distance. He used to hitch rides and walk some distance that is all. But that does not undermine his passion for the game.'

Kavitha believed Shivanna was right, though she did not like the truth. *'That somehow made Rohit a lesser person'* she thought. *'I will ask him about this, one of these days.'*

'One of such rides he got was in my car. It was quite accidental. I was a bit drunk that day also. I used to have a farmhouse further down on Kanakapura road. On that day, I had taken couple of friends to the farmhouse and we had a nice boozing session. As we were returning, we noticed the young boy walking hurriedly towards the city.' He was gesturing to every passing vehicle, for a free ride to the city.'

Kavitha was completely engrossed in the story. She was no longer hoping that Rohit's interview would end fast and he would return to attend to Shivanna. She liked stories; especially about the legend, that her husband was.

'We would not have even looked at him a second time as we drove along, if not for something he had in his raised hand, while asking for a lift.'

'What was it?'

'It would have been commonplace, if it were with any of the city lads. But in the hands of a ragged village urchin, it looked totally out of place. It was a five hundred rupees test match entry ticket for the Karnataka State Cricket Association stadium. Mind you, that was the last day of a test match between India and Australia. One of the friends in my car, a member of the State Cricket Association, instantly recognized the ticket. He was curious to know, how the boy got the ticket.'

We were so stupid, he said to himself. We did not expect the boy to even know what the colored piece of paper meant . . . how wrong we were!

Kavitha wondered why the narrator all of a sudden went silent. She was in a hurry to hear the story before Rohit returned.

'So you gave him a lift?' she asked.

'No, not that fast. We stopped the car near him and asked him where he wanted to go. Those days also, he had the same expressionless face. He said *Kasturba Road*.'

'Kasturba Road! Why?' Kavitha asked.

'KSACA stadium is actually at the meeting point of Kasturba Road and M.G. Road. He was right about asking for a lift to Kasturba Road. '

'Then you allowed him in?'

'Come on, we were not in a mood to give in without some fun. First, the KSCA fellow offered him a thousand rupees for the ticket. He flatly refused. In those days, thousand rupees would have been big money for him. To add to that, the last day's play was expected to last only a few minutes with Australia on the edge of an easy victory. I do not think too many people would have ventured to the ground to watch the match, which was to end in less than an hour.'

'Probably Rohit may not have known that,' Kavitha thought she needed to defend Rohit's naiveté somehow.

'No, he knew. We even tried to explain to him the game would end in an hour and those thousand rupees were a bargain for him; but the guy refused!'

'He must have been really passionate about the game!'

'He was. We finally gave him a lift. But my KSCA friend was still curious about how he got the ticket. So, we asked him, that was the most interesting part,' Shivanna stopped as he reminisced the moment.

'He had been standing outside the cricket stadium gate for the last four days, without a way to get inside. Then on the fourth day, he had found someone who did not have any plans to watch the final day. So, our boy got the ticket, which he carried like a treasure, as a gift from someone who had better plans than to watch the last one hour of a boring game. That was one of the many games where India was beaten comprehensively by the Aussies.'

Kavitha sat imagining the young Rohit standing near the gates for days without any possibility of getting in, the very same gates, which would now have red carpets when he walked in.

'So, you dropped him at the stadium, that day?'

'Yes we did. Then I started noticing him on the road many times, as I traveled back and forth to my farmhouse. I got to know him better, about him and his family. They were all very good people. I have watched him struggling for his game and for his family. He has always been a nice, loving guy, you know.'

'I know Shivanna,' Kavitha said. He is much more than a nice person; he is a gem!

She felt her repulsion to Shivanna melting away. Still she did not approve the shoes in the house or drinking. Above everything, she knew Shivanna had come in to seek some financial favor and she did not approve that at all.

Rahul is very generous with money, she thought.

'Shivanna, please tell me more about him, his life . . . those days.'

Shivanna laughed a hearty laugh this time.

'You adore him, don't you?' He asked with a wicked but playful grin on his face.

'Yes I do,' she responded shyly.

Before Shivanna could start what he was about to say, Rohit came in hurriedly and closed the door behind him.

'Shivanna . . . oh great . . . you do not look sloshed any more. So tell me how you are feeling now,' Rohit failed to camouflage his concern.

Shivanna's playful face changed. He got up and walked about with a serious brooding expression on his face.

'Rohit, son, I need a favor from you and you cannot say no to this.'

'Tell me, you know I would do anything in my capacity.'

'It is not much Rohit. Something, very simple for you. In the first Innings tomorrow, you have to get out without scoring a single run,' he said without looking at Rohit's face.

Though delivered inconspicuously, it was obvious that it took a great effort for him to say what he wanted.

'What?' Rohit asked.

'Yes you have to throw your wicket away with no run on score board.'

Before Rohit could reply, there was a knock on the door.

'Rohit, we are leaving, we just wanted to say bye and wish you all the very best for tomorrow's test.' The television anchor, holding a bunch of gadgets, bid goodbye.

She did not realize, until much later, that she had forgotten to switch off her telescopic sound recorder after the video session. It had recorded the last few sentences from the room, without her knowing, while she waited near the door deciding whether to knock at the door for a final best wishes or not.

Rohit quickly, yet courteously accepted the wishes and closed the door behind him. Then, he heaved a sigh of relief.

'Shivanna...what did you just say? Have you gone mad?' Rohit's raised his voice.

'No Rohit, this is my last chance. My creditors are after me. if I do not pay within this week, they would kill me.'

'So you decided to bet on me? Why didn't you ask me for money instead? I would have given you enough to hang on.'

'You know it Rohit, the debt is over five crores. You do not have that kind of money to throw away. Even if you have, I would not take it.'

So!' Rohit's voice was still edgy.

'I created all that burden with my foolishness . . . horses and cricket, damn betting, only I am to blame for it. I am betting one last time, to repay all my debts. I will never do it again.'

'You think I would ever do what you are asking me . . . ever in my life?'

'No Rohit, you won't normally. You are too good a human being to cheat, even if it is in a game. But look at me. This is life or death situation for me. I have borrowed a huge sum already and put all that money on you, on your scoring a "*duck*[7]" tomorrow. Why? Because that is the only way for me to pay back everything. You can do it, you can do it for me, you can easily do it for me . . . not as a repayment for anything but out of love.' Shivanna was already in tears.

'Rohit, I am completely ashamed to ask you this. While I am asking you this favor, I am dying a thousand deaths. But this is the only time . . . only once in my lifetime, I am going to ask you a favor, a favor to save a dying man.'

Kavitha stood silent, waiting for Rohit's reaction.

Rohit was unmoved.

'Shivanna, nothing can make me do what you are asking.'

'Rohit, think about it for a second. You do not lose anything. You just have to make sure that you are out without scoring a run. It is easy, just miss a ball, allow yourself to be bowled; or give a catch to someone or run for an impossible single and get yourself out. No one will know.'

'Shivanna, Rohit was about to say something when Shivanna's phone rang.

---

[7] Duck - a common term used in cricket for getting out without scoring any run.

He looked at the phone; saw the number and his face turned white.

'Mehboob Bhai,' he said.

Rohit signaled him to answer the call.

Shivanna picked the phone and walked to the adjacent room, listening and nodding without saying much.

He looked completely scared.

'Rohit, why are you even considering such a preposterous demand?' Kavitha said it as soon as Shivanna was out of earshot.

'You should just call the police. Match fixing is a crime. This guy should be behind the bars,' she continued.

Rohit looked at her without saying anything. She noticed that his normally emotionless face had traces of pain on it.

'Rohit, whatever it is, tell me,' she demanded.

Rohit did not answer. His continued to look at her face but his mind was obviously somewhere else.

She moved closer to him, shook him a bit and said, 'Rohit, you are forgetting that you have a wife now. Tell me, why you tolerate such ridiculous demands from people? Who is this Shivanna? I know he has given you a few lifts to the stadium; may be a little more than that. Why do you act so indebted to him?'

Even that did not evoke much response from Rohit.

'How close is he to you? He did not even attend our wedding. We have been married for over three weeks now. I have never heard him giving you even a call all these days. We have reached Bangalore almost a week back and he has not met us till today.'

'He was in a de-addiction center for the last two months - for alcoholics - purely on my insistence,' Rohit added.

'OK, that explains why I have not met him. Now, all of a sudden, how can he walk in fully drunk, gets treated like a king in my home and demand outrageous favors. Who is he? Why are you reluctant to call the police?'

This time Rohit opened his mouth as if to say something but decided against it.

'Rohit . . . I am talking to you. Are you going to answer me?' Kavitha was losing patience.

'Shivanna told me everything about his relation with you. How he met you as a child, how he helped you reach the stadium once and how he witnessed your growth and so on. You need not have to be so grateful to him for all that. You are being too soft, sweetheart.''

This time Rohit spoke.

'He told you nothing Kavitha. He will never tell you, or anyone for that matter, all that he had done for me. He is too nice a person to discuss the help he has given.' His voice was stern and calm.

It was Kavitha's turn to be silent, an uneasy silence born out of shock.

'Kavitha, I do not know what he had told you. But I can tell you that is all true. It was only a small part of the whole story, though. You know Shivanna is a man who has failed in life because he is too good a human being. When you saw the man first time, almost demanding his way in here, what did you think about him?'

'I thought he was a rich guy, lacking manners to have dropped in drunk and demand a meeting with you. I had tried to send him off. But he said, on hearing his name, you would come running to meet him. Looks like he knows you, much better than I have understood you so far.' There was jealousy in Kavitha's voice.

'After hearing his demand now, what is your opinion of him?' Rohit asked her.

'Oh, now? I think he is a rich man turned pauper, thanks to some expensive life style or some major vices. He already talked about betting on horses and cricket. Enough to bring one down. And he seems shameless and criminal too, to have asked you such an absurd favor.'

'Kavitha, I will tell you about Shivanna. He was indeed a very rich man, having inherited a fortune from his father. But that was quite some time back. He did his graduation in social work and worked with an NGO for some time. A few years later, he decided to use most of his money in building a multi-specialty hospital in a village in North Karnataka. The hospital was expected to be a non-profit enterprise.'

'You mean Shivanna started a hospital for rural folks?'

'Yes, the hospital was a big success and people all over North Karnataka flocked to his hospital since the treatment was almost free. But that left a gaping hole in Shivanna's pocket. And when he found it impossible to fund the day-to-day operations of the hospital, he donated it to a religious organization , a *mutt*[8].'

'He donated the whole hospital! I cannot believe it,' exclaimed Kavitha,

'I am telling you Shivanna is different. After that, with reduced financial power, Shivanna started a real estate company, which never really took off. The first piece of land his company bought landed him in the court. Lengthy court proceedings and the inevitable loss of all his investment finally broke his spirit. He took to drinking.'

---

[8] Mutt - A Hindu monastic and/or religious establishment with a lineage, which has rules and is hierarchical. It is the short form of the word Matha.

'Your first meeting happened after he was brought down to that shape?'

'Yes, he had a farmhouse in Kaggalipura those days; his only possession, other than the house he lived in!'

'What about his wife and children?'

'His wife had died of cancer a few years after their marriage. The hospital was built in her memory. It was his *Taj Mahal* for her. They did not have any children'

Kavitha started feeling some sympathy for the man who loved his wife so much that he spent all his fortune to build a hospital in her name.

'His friends were still those people who treated him like rich, who drank with his money and laughed at his expense. He understood them but never detested or avoided them. After our first meeting, we met often, and a strange bond developed between us. I guess he was impressed by the village boy who had an unwavering passion called cricket, and the boy was impressed with the rich man's large heart.'

'Was your interactions limited to hitching rides to the stadium?'

'No. It went much beyond that. The rich man sponsored the boy for a thirty-day camp at the Brijesh Patel Academy[9]. That is where I learnt the techniques of batting.'

'Aha, he funded you! But he never mentioned that!'

'I am not surprised. That is Shivanna. Eventually, I do not know when, my success became his obsession. He sent me to Australian Cricket Academy for a six months course, which was a finishing school of sorts for young cricketers, those days.

---

[9] A world class cricket academy run by an ex-test cricketer

When I came back, I realized he had to sell his farmhouse to fund my trip.'

'He sold his farm house to help you!'

'He did indeed. Do not be too surprised. He often tells I am the son he never had.'

'Did he help you again any time?'

'Three years back, during my first season playing for Karnataka, I suffered a severe injury in my right ankle. A complicated surgery only could have saved my career. Poor as we were, I was facing oblivion. But Shivanna turned up with the required money to send me to UK for a series of surgeries. He raised the money for my surgeries by pledging his house.'

'I can't believe it!'' Kavitha exclaimed.

'No one would. But for Shivanna, as I said, I was and am the son he always wanted. We are the family he yearns for.''

'How did he run up debt in crores? Was that for you?' Kavitha wished he would say *not for me*.

'I wouldn't say so. He sold his farmhouse and pretty much lost his house for me. But the huge debt was of his own making. From the time, his wife died, he had spent a lot of time and money on some worthless friends. They introduced the world of betting to him. This was in addition to alcoholism'

'Betting?'

'Yes, initially it was for fun. He betted on single digit daily lotteries, which offered eight times the return if you guessed the day's number correct. That did not involve much money; did not provide much thrill either. Then he moved on to bigger stuff, like horseracing. There, the stakes were much higher and so where the losses. To feed his appetite, he started borrowing - borrowing from people with black money and mafia connections.'

'Aha, that explains!

'It did not stop there. He found betting on cricket matches, even more rewarding, rewarding not only in terms of money but also in terms of thrill as well. Shivanna always considered himself a cricket aficionado any way. So, here was a field, where he could make educated bets, unlike racing. That was what he thought and he was completely wrong.'

'Why?'

'Because, many times, the outcomes of matches were doctored. Where matches produced results based on merit, Shivanna often predicted correctly. But the returns were minimal as the outcome was as per the expectations of the betting fraternity. In betting, you make money if you bet on some event no one expects to happen.'

'So now Shivanna wants to you to doctor an outcome - your score in the first innings - to make up for all his losses because everyone expects you to do well? Has he approached you before?' Kavitha asked in an edgy voice. 'Never. . . . that is what worries me. I know Shivanna's love for the game. That would never permit him to even think in these terms, unless he is in deep trouble. More than that, he as a person would never resort to cheating unless his life was in danger. I suspect he is telling the truth, he is already out of time!'

'What are you going to do? Would you cheat for him?'

'I do not know. I owe everything I have, to him. His timely assistance made me what I am today. He sacrificed everything he had for my career. Had it not for him, I would still have been working in the same brick factory where my brother worked once. I owe him my life.'

'But Rohit, you owe your life to Cricket too. Also, there are values you need to consider.'

'What values? Nobody would have helped me with money when I needed it. I would not have been where I am, if I had expected the society, which puts so much of stress on values, to help me. What Shivanna did was also against the same values you are talking about, - selling one's house to fund some stray kid's love for a game! That was strictly against the society's norms, the society's values.'

'But that did not harm anyone.'

'Oh yes, no harm to anyone. My getting out without scoring also would not harm anyone. Even if the team loses the match, no one is going to lose sleep. After all, it is a game, not war. I have scored consecutive fifties in the last six innings including two centuries. I can afford a *duck* now. I have produced more that what was expected of me this year.'

'But Rohit . . .'

'There is no *but* here. It is not a crime if I scored a zero this time. Anyway, the law of averages would soon catch up with me. I am bound to score a *duck* soon, in the normal scheme of things. A deliberate *duck* is against the norm, I agree. But so was what Shivanna had done for me.'

'So, you are going to oblige?'

Before Rohit could answer, Shivanna came back. His face was flushed, and he was sweating.

'Rohit . . . that was the ultimatum. They will kill me if I do not repay this week.'

'Shivanna, what have you got yourself into? What have you got us into? Have you really placed a bet on my scoring a duck?' Rohit asked.

'Yes, I had borrowed seventy-five lakhs and put the entire amount on your getting out without scoring in the first innings; the return is fourteen times!'

Rohit was silent for minutes. Shivanna looked at him eagerly. *There is a ray of hope*, he thought.

'Shivanna, I owe you everything I have. You can take all my assets and repay the loans you have. It would be much more than your debts. I have a long career ahead. We can make up everything we lose now.'

Kavitha was stunned. She did not expect Rohit to make such an offer.

'What if he accepts?' she wondered.

'Rohit that is not an acceptable solution. I do not want your money.' Shivanna acted as if that was the indecent proposal.

'That is not my money. We made it together. I would not have made anything without your timely help.'

'No Rohit, you made that through your skill, dedication, and hard work. I won't allow that to fund a fool's crazy addiction to betting.'

'But you had spent all your money on a foolish kid's crazy addiction to the game, that wasn't wrong?'

'No it wasn't . . . the great *Destroyer* standing in front of me proves that.'

'Then why not?'

'No Rohit, forget it. If you cannot do what I have requested, tell me. I would understand. I will respect your decision. I will never blame you for what happens to me after that.'

Rohit did not say anything.

'Tell me whether you would do it or not, say *Yes* or *No*.'

Rohit was quiet for a few minutes. His face was still expressionless but Kavitha could feel the storm brewing in his heart.

This silence was deafening.

Then he exploded without losing the calm composure in his voice.

'Shivanna, I will quit the game today. I will not play the match tomorrow and never again. But I cannot cheat in my game. This is final.' Rohit's voice had steel in it.

'Hey, don't go down that path, son. You did not work so hard to just reach the top and then throw it away. I would not allow that. It is fine. I will accept the fate awaiting me. I am proud that I have spent a good part of my life nurturing a great cricketer and more than that, a perfect human being.' He turned to face the door to cover up the tears rolling down his cheeks.

'God bless you son, and good luck,' he said as he walked towards the door.

Rohit broke down in a sudden burst of emotions. His knees gave way and he slumped on the floor.

He shouted . . .

"Shivanna, you go wherever you want to; To meet whatever fate awaits you. But remember, you refused to accept a workable solution and demand the impossible from me. You came here to ask for your *pound of flesh*. I won't give you that. I will not cheat. You watch tomorrow, I will score, not just score, I will give my life to score a century. I am telling you, *a century*, the best in my career . . . even if I have to kill for it. You go and get lost; you can't have your pound of flesh. Shivanna, how could you ever ask me to score a duck?'

Then he cried like a child.

Your pound of flesh! Echoed in Shivanna's mind.

He was shattered. Never the less, he collected himself fast and as he walked out of the house, he took his mobile from the trouser pocket and dialed a number.' Hello this is Shivanna, ah yes, Shivanna Gowda. Remember, the seventy-five lakhs I had betted on Rohit Shenoy scoring a *duck*? I just want to change it. No, not canceling it, I am just changing it. Yes . . . yes, change it to *his scoring over fifty runs* in the first innings. Yes, I understand the return is only seven times. That is fine. Oh no, no . . . I don't have any inside info. I will sign the papers tomorrow before the start of the game.'

As an unusual peace and calmness descended on him. He realized his absolute trust in Rohit's determination and skill might save him, after all, that too without bringing any disgrace to the great cricketer or the game.

As he slept peacefully in the night, after many months, a just married cricketer and his wife spent the whole night without sleep, thanks to the emotional turmoil, he had caused.

As India won the toss and elected to bat, Rohit tried to catch up some sleep, sitting in the players' area. *The openers are capable of spending at least couple of hours in the middle,* he thought. He did not expect, as the one down batsman, his services to be in demand any time soon.

He was drifting to a catnap when his phone rang. He saw Shivanna's number and he immediately disconnected it. The previous day's incidents quickly rushed back to his mind.

'I will definitely score a hundred,' he muttered under his breath.

The score was sixty-five for no loss with just over thirty minutes to go for lunch break, when disaster stuck. Opener Surinder

Singh took off for a non-existent single to be marooned in no man land while Matt O'Neill broke his stumps with a direct throw. The score moved to sixty-five for one.

The crowd broke into a warm applause as Rohit walked towards the crease casually, yet trying to loosen his arms by rotating it.

The crowd wanted the *destroyer* to do his job.

He took his mark and looked around.

This is the last ball of the over. I need to be calm and build a solid foundation before moving on to attack mode, he tried to calm his nerves.

But, after a long time since he started his international career, he felt extremely nervous.

As Dilley started his long run up, Rohit felt his heart beating faster and faster. He took a deep breath and told himself, *Rohit, do not do anything reckless, defend the ball'*

As the ball hit the pitch and bounced up, Rohit used a straight bat trying to bring the ball to a standstill.

'That was a slow moving gift of a delivery asking to be hit. But the *destroyer* seems to be sleep walking here. He tried to go forward and defended the ball, which was short pitched outside the off stump. This does not augur well for India' - The Australian commentator who had a 'thing' against all playing cricketers, irrespective of their country or predicted for the millions of viewers..

Kavitha cringed as she watched Rohit's mistake on the forty-seven inch television screen at home.

'Eighty three percent of the time Rohit had missed connecting the first ball, he has gone on to score fifty plus,' added the statistician in the commentary box fiddling with the keys on his laptop.

Kavitha felt better. So did Shivanna who was watching the game in his hotel room.

The next over from Dave was eventless as Rohit's partner defended the balls dourly. But on the fifth ball, he managed to score a single by tapping it on the onside and left Rohit to face the last one.

Rohit took his mark deliberately, slowly. He wanted to calm his nerves, which had never affected him all these years, at least like now.

Rohit, play your natural game, his mind said. You are not a defensive player. Go on the offense.

Dave's last ball was an in swinger aimed close to the batsman's feet and was at perfect good length. Rohit stepped out of the crease and hit it hard.

'Wow, that was a massive hit, though mistimed. It was a gem of a delivery. Anybody other than Rohit Shenoy would have respected the ball and the bowler and bent their knees in forward defense; but not the *destroyer*. He danced down the crease and hit it high and hard to the vacant area. He should get a run here.' The Indian commentator, who had taken over, shouted over the television microphone at the top of his voice.

His partner egged Rohit to run. But Rohit did not hear him. He was in another world, in a trance.

'Look at that, Rohit Shenoy has let go of that easy run to avoid strike in the next over. He seems to have decided to avoid Dilley at least in the initial overs and concentrate on Dave. With Dilley bowling at a much better line and length, a great strategy to take on the Aussies today. Anyway, he has already made his intentions clear in the last ball. Watch out Dave' Even the commentators were excited.

Dilley's next over was a maiden. It was Rohit's turn again and Dave decided to go round the wicket at him.

Rohit again tried to calm his nerves. I need to open account somehow. Otherwise, I would get more and more worried and do something drastic to lose my wicket.

I will hit the first ball itself for a four, he decided.

Dilley's first ball was fast and it hit Rohit's pads. His premediated heave was too far away from the ball.

'Oooooooh,' the audience exclaimed.

The next ball was a slower one and despite the best efforts, he could not connect. The wicket keeper collected it neatly.

Rohit panicked. He tried to exorcise Shivanna's image from his mind.

Crowd jeered, and the jeering grew louder with each ball he missed.

The fifth was the fastest in that over so far. Rohit had already faced six balls in the game connecting just one and looking like an idiot with the rest.

He was overcautious as he faced the fifth ball of the over. It was a *Yorker*. It found a gaping hole between his raised bat and lean body and landed right on his stumps. At close to hundred miles an hour, it broke the left stump.

It shattered his mind as well.

As he walked back to the pavilion, slouched, the crowd booed.

Kavitha moved away from the television.

Shivanna watched the scene in disbelief. His world shattered around him.

He was wrong!

He had made serious mistakes!

In fact, two of them!

One was changing the bet he had initially placed.

The other, more important, unpardonable one was concerning Rohit.

He immediately dialed Rohit's number.

No answer.

'Rohit, please pick up the phone. Oh God, please make him accept, just this call.' he prayed silently.

Rohit did not.

He knew there was no point in trying. Rohit would not.

He keyed in a text message for Rohit and read it many times before sending.

Then, without waiting for any response from Rohit, he picked up the licensed pistol he always carried.

Rohit sat at the player's area with his head bowed. It was not the first *duck* in his career. But, today, he felt summarily defeated.

His mobile rang. He disconnected it seeing Shivanna's number.

He was ashamed; ashamed at his own failure.

He did not want to talk to anyone, especially Shivanna.

Then he received a text message from Shivanna.

He opened it slowly without really wanting to read it.

It read, Son, I misread your love for me.

Rohit hated the message, whatever it meant. More than that, he hated Shivanna.

Post lunch session saw Indian team consolidating with one of the openers going on to score a century.

It was getting closer to teatime. The team physiotherapist walked in and asked Rohit to come out of the pavilion.

Then he broke the news to him; the news about a certain Shivanna killing himself using a licensed pistol in one of the city hotels!

Rahul felt as if a hammer had hit him. When sense came back to him, he was at his doorstep. There was an unusually large contingent of television crew outside. As he reached the door braving the media men who were shouting at him all kinds of questions which he could not understand, Kavitha came running.

She seemed to have been crying for a long time! May be she knows about Shivanna by now, he thought.

As they walked towards the very sofa where Shivanna sat the previous day, the television showed the day's breaking news.

They watched in horror, as the sound clip of Shivanna requesting Rohit to get out without scoring any run, interlaced with Rohit getting bowled by a Dilley delivery, as requested, showed up on the television screen.

Biggest match fixing in Indian cricket exposed, - claimed the familiar television anchor.

'The way Rohit tackled every ball he had faced, including his refusal to run a sure run which was there for the asking, proves the conspiracy beyond doubt,' explained one of the experts.

Rohit crouched on the floor and wept uncontrollably.

The *destroyer* was completely destroyed.

He felt a soft tap on his shoulders. As he turned, the crying face of his life partner told him silently, Rohit, I understand you...

She saw in front of her, a man who would never sell his country or his game, even to avoid his own destruction. She hugged him tightly.

The stone pelting by irate fans at the glass windows started soon. But to Rohit, it felt like rain droplets falling to wash away his worries as he sank his face in her lap and cried.

With her at his side, another sunny day was not far off, he felt; because true love is much more valuable than the game, fame, money, and success.

****

Judges of Human Character

'I hate this guy,' Tom George, the ace film director announced while leafing through the latest edition of the 'Film Magazine.'

His finger was pointing to a badly printed picture of one of the upcoming actors.

'You know him?' I asked with a tone of disbelief, more so to butter Tom's ego, than to take the conversation forward. *Obviously, someone of Tom's pedigree would definitely know the actor.*

'Oh yes, of course, he has acted in two of Palatt sir's movies. I used to be his assistant director then.'

Tom was an assistant to the legendary filmmaker Raju Palatt for ages, I knew. When most of his peers, graduated from 'assisting' to 'leading' roles in the director profession, Tom stuck around with his guru, till the guru decided to call it a day. But with two back-to-back hits, that too with movies which he had not only directed but penned also, Tom had climbed the ratings in no time, to reach the very top in less than two years.

'His name used to be Dennis those days, much before he became "Rising Star" Padmakumar. He was one of the many who used to frequent shooting locations looking for a role.' We had just started our journey from Cochin. Our packed SUV had the ace director and couple of his assistants and a production manager as co passengers. For some reason, the assistants and the production manager observed reverential silence in front of Tom.

Sandhya, my wife, as usual, was at the wheel but was unusually quiet during this trip. Anjali my third grade daughter made herself comfortable with an iPod in the back seat.

We had a long way to go.

'After a lot of pleading, the production manager in one of Palatt sir's movies, I think it was the successful movie 'Admiral', agreed to give this guy a role; a negligible role, in the movie. Armed with the confidence of just one scene, one day, he walked up to me and greeted me. One look at the guy, I knew he would be a lousy actor. I had even told it to the production manager then. You know, I can recognize a good actor from a thousand kilometers,' Tom paused for effect.

I could not believe that somebody so revered could be as boastful.

'But he has matured as an actor. I have heard that he is being considered for the national award this year,' I tried to deflate Tom a bit.

'Oh yah, you heard right. He would not get that though. There is an equally bad actor from Hindi vying for this years' award. He is bound to get it. If this guy gets a national award, we serious film makers would all look like clowns. Such a "full of himself guy," and a bad actor too.' Tom gave an impression that he would be shattered if 'Dennis' got the award.

'I remember clearly. This guy was the butt of a joke that time' Tom seemed hell-bent on destroying the young star's reputation, at least among us.

The assistant director and I were all ears. Sandhya sprang to attention as she deftly handled a sharp curve; I knew she would not lose an opportunity to listen to gossip, that too about a famous actor. Even Anju was interested.

'The opening scene in 'Admiral', if you remember, was a large mob chasing the villain. Then there was a close up of the mob. Camera pans on the faces of five-six people in the mob, they are supposed to be common men and not major characters in the movie, and stops at the hero's face, with a zoom in. That was how the movie started.'

I did remember the movie. It was a huge commercial success. The villain was the distilled version of all the vices, a political king maker and hero an angry young man wronged by the system, which was controlled and manipulated by the villain.

'One of the six faces in the mob was our Dennis. We shot that scene on the second or the third day. The same scene repeats at the climax of the movie. This time the camera pans back on the same six faces and then on to the scared villain tied to a post. Then as expected in every Indian movie, the hero hacks the villain to death, in some form of jungle justice.' Tom stopped a second allowing as to re-run the scenes in our minds' eye.

'Our Dennis did not have any other scene in the movie. He was expected to be present at the climax scene for just that one shot. Considering the dates of some senior actors, the climax scene was scheduled three days later. '

I tried to imagine the poor fellow hanging around the location for days together to appear in the last shot as well.

'But after the first shot, our friend started acting like a super star. Before the climax shot, he demanded some money from the production manager.'

'For what?' the assistant asked.

'He said, "When the camera pans back, if my face is not there, you would be in trouble. If you do not pay me wages in advance, I would walk out..."'

'Interesting,' I said, thinking laterally on how I could have solved such a problem.

'Then?'

'Palatt sir overheard him and he threw him out of the set without even thinking twice.'

'How did you manage without him? Did you re-shoot the first sequence?' I asked.

'No, we couldn't do that. The hero had already left the location. The scene after the camera panning back on to the villain's face was to be shot indoors in the studio.'

'So Dennis blackmailed you knowing all that?'

'I guess so.'

'How did you manage?'

'Come on. We had hundred ways of solving the problem. It was too simple. Dennis was fortunately the last one in the line. Palatt sir said, "*Instead of six faces, we would show five.*" Then he mercilessly edited Dennis out. We all used to laugh about the guy's temerity for quite some time.'

'But he is now flying high,' I said as if to poke a hole into Tom's assertions.

'Yes he is, too much luck and too little talent,' Tom remarked sarcastically.

'I am telling you, I realized he did not have any acting in his blood, the very first time I had seen him. You know I can feel talent.'

I hoped sincerely that he would not repeat this dialog throughout the journey. After all, his heroes had a tendency to repeat some phrases to drill their characters in the mind of the audience.

Sandhya, who was silent all this while, just to cut short Tom's boasting suddenly asked, 'Sir, where do you want me to stop for lunch?'

I , being the most regular traveler on Cochin-Bangalore road, within the group, suggested. 'Let us stop at Salem. Some nice restaurants have come up there in the last couple of years.'

'Ashokji, next time you should write a story about these border areas' Tom said looking at the serene villages, as we entered the Kerala-Tamil Nadu border. 'I am sure; they have a number of stories to tell with the leftist culture seeping in from Kerala conflicting with their Dravidian feudalism.'

I did not say anything but I knew the great reader of thespian faces could read my thoughts effortlessly.

'I wish you used some village in *Coimbatore* instead of '*Vidurashwatha*' in the story,' he said referring to my story '*Picking out the bad one - A question on Morals*' included in my first book.

'Surveying the location would have been easier,' he continued.

We were on a trip to survey the location for a movie based on that story; my first film making experience. One of my friends in the advertising industry had gifted a copy of my book to a film producer and he felt that '*A question on Morals*' had all the *masala* for a commercial film.

Tom, who had the dates of a superstar and being a super director himself, naturally became the obvious choice for the director role.

As Tom and I started working on the screenplay, it dawned on us that visiting *'Vidurashwatha'*, where the story was centered, could make things easier. We even hoped to stay there for couple of weeks to iron out the script.

That is why we got in our SUV and drove north on that sunny May morning.

Soon the conversation changed to various characters in the story and who in the Malayalam film industry could fit in what role. Tom surprised me with his mastery over the movie classics from all over the world. He talked at length about how Akira Kurosawa to Steven Spielberg would have presented each of my characters while I wondered where all those dimensions came from.

'Ashokji, you should have told the story from the Indian Father's perspective.' The master director hammered the final nail in my story.

It was getting warm outside; inside too. We had reached Salem.

I had a nice hotel, Hotel Sharavana Bhavan - in mind.

As we passed one of the thatched teashops, Tom suddenly shouted,' stop . . . stop.'

'We are stopping here for lunch,' he declared.

'Here?' I asked unable to register the suggestion.

The restaurant was not really a restaurant. The unclean board hanging precariously at the front read *'Hotel Gold'*, But the 'G' in the board was so worn out that it easily be read as *'Hotel old'* which probably was more appropriate.

Spelling errors in the prominently displayed menu convinced me later, that the mistake in the name was not purposeful and was not meant to be a forewarning. How else could there be

'Rise', 'Green Piece', 'pups' on the menu.

'Here?' I asked again.

The assistant directors looked at me with amusement. After all, they knew their boss and his quirks.

I avoided Sandhya's eyes as I considered the aftermath of our feasting here.

'Ashokji, you should visit such places . . . places frequented by common folks, only there you would meet real characters, for real stories. Stories with the smell of the soil.''

Stories or no stories, I could see food with the smell of the soil and surroundings with the smell of cow dung. I did not cherish either even for a moment.

'Dad, we cannot be eating here,' Anju boldly put forth her point.

When it comes to being candid, you can never beat children. They are never tied down by respect or fear.

'Why not, Anju? It would build character,'' Tom blunted Anju's objection.

I immediately suspected Tom probably liked *Calvin and Hobbs*.

'Tom sir is always like this. Such adventures give him an opportunity to understand and realistically depict village scenes in his movies,' One of the assistants whispered in my ears.

'Will he also eat food in such places?' I asked, still not believing such an eventuality.

'Oh, he does, .he always says that one needs to experience the reality to paint it on the screen,' the assistant continued his whispering.

I thanked god that my story did not call for prison scene or police harassment. I did not want to be around when the great director decided to experience those firsthand.

As we walked closer, I saw a beggar sitting with a child under an old Neem tree. An Aluminum plate sat in front of him on a dirty towel and there were a few coins in it. The kid pleaded with his eyes, saying more without saying anything.

I extracted a few coins from my pocket, and dropped them in the plate without thinking.

Tom looked at me and looked at the beggar as if he could extract some real soil-smelling story from the scene. Then he walked towards the restaurant entrance with a wry smile.

I wondered what he found amusing.

As we sat on the makeshift benches and ordered 'Rice' and '*Sambhar* ', we realized that the menu hanging there was more of a showpiece. Only what we ordered was really available. 'What do you think about that guy?' Tom asked pointing to the beggar outside, as we waited for the food to arrive.

'What is there to think?' I replied with a counter question.

'I mean, as an author, look at that beggar and tell me what you see.'

'A man of about forty five, begging for a lively hood. That kid may be his son and the mother may be begging somewhere else. May be there are younger children as well. Every evening they would bring their earnings to some illegally built hut on some government land where they cook nutrition-less porridge, satiate their hunger with it and catch sleep under a non-existent roof.' I concluded the 'author's view' of the beggar's world.

'And . . . ?' Tom was not the one to let me go so easily.

'And . . . and they would dream of their son growing up into a bigger, better and more successful beggar because they are not licensed to dream of riches and a better life,' I said caustically.

'Why?' another monosyllable question.

'Because, the haves are hoarding all there is and the have-nots can only die a wretched life,' I said pleased with my description ' *die a wretched life'.*', which was obviously better than saying *'live a wretched life.'*

'But you have missed something important Ashokji. Have a closer look at the guy.'

I was in no mood to get up and have a closer look at the guy; but I realized that I had taken something for granted thus missing the complete picture. The beggar was sitting on a small stool like contraption with wheels. His legs were folded and were apparently useless. He was handicapped and could not stand or walk on his powerless limbs.

'Oh yes, I missed out the handicap. The guy is stuck on that contraption and that explains the presence of his son here. Otherwise, my story holds.' I said digging my hand into the heap of hot rice, which had just arrived in front of me.

'I will show you something interesting, after the meals' remarked Tom as he attacked his plate mercilessly.

One needed to be quite aggressive and adventurous in life to be attacking that meal in these surroundings, I thought to myself as I started testing my tolerance.

I watched Sandhya through the corner of my eyes. She too was trying to eat what was in front of her with great difficulty. Anju, on the other hand, was feasting on it as if she had not seen food for days.

As we paid the bill and walked out after the forgettable meal, Tom lit a cigarette.

'Quite some time back, Palatt sir and I met a similar beggar sitting by the road, another disabled person like the beggar we saw outside the hotel.' He started the story, blowing rings of smoke in the air. He had a dazed look on his face, his eyes seemed to be fixed on some distant spot, fixed somewhere in the past.

I hoped that Tom's new story would not end with the beggar growing into one of my favorite stars, thanks to Palatt sir's Midas touch.

'You know Palatt sir's movies are unique in his treatment and creation of characters.'

Oh yes, you just created one for us, by making us eat here, I told myself.

'Palatt sir called the guy aside showed him a hundred rupee note and told him, *"I would give this to you if you get up and run to that tree."*'

I was flabbergasted. How could someone be so rude and demeaning to a fellow human being, that too, a handicapped beggar!

'That is interesting, what happened then?' the production manager asked.

'He initially protested. Then Palatt sir added one more hundred, and that sealed it!'

We all looked at each other.

'Yes, the guy got up and ran as if his life depended on it!'

'He was not disabled? He was a fraud!' I asked without believing what Tom said.

'Yes he was. Both his legs were fine. He, in fact, came back walking for the money, without any shame or remorse on his face. Palatt sir promptly paid the money.'

'What? You should have reported him to the police.' my obsession with integrity poured forth. *After all, integrity should be integrity, even if you are a beggar.*

'No ,not at all,'' Tom said.

'So you guys paid money like fools!'?'

'No, not like fools but as sensible businessmen. Palatt sir felt Rs.200 was too low a price for a great comical incident which he could weave into one of his movies.'

'Huh, oh that makes sense.' I climbed down from my high moral ground, defeated.

'Did he use that part in any of his films?'

'He did not, but I think one of his friends did.'

Taking the last puff from the dying cigarette, Tom beckoned the beggar's boy to approach him.

The boy came driving an imaginary auto-rickshaw.[10]

'Bring your dad here, and I will give you ten rupees.' Tom commanded majestically, dangling a ten-rupee note.

'Let us try the same trick on this guy,' Tom whispered as the boy ran to his father.

Though I was taken aback by the beggar's deceptions, I did not want Tom to try the same thing again. . *After all, what new story could be revealed here? Who was he to play with human minds especially of the less privileged ones?*

I guess neither the assistants nor the production manager looked forward to it either.

The kid pushed his father carefully on the stool like contraption and brought it to a hasty stop near us.

For the first time, I noticed the beggar at close quarters.

He was disheveled. His eyes looked at me as if to seek an escape from his miseries. His legs were folded back on the seat and the

---

[10] Auto rickshaw - a three wheeled vehicle used for public transport in India

arms held the Aluminum plate as if it was the most precious possession he ever had. His clothes were torn and soiled and the wrinkles on his face and the sun-tanned skin advertised the minimal but fighting existence he had.

I knew he was not pretending to be a disabled person. Even if he was, I did not want him to be humbled any more. Somehow, I felt that we have no right to inflict additional wounds on his battered soul.

I wanted Tom to be wrong. I guess, all of us wanted it.

'Hey, what is your father's name?' Tom asked the kid as he handed over the promised ten-rupee note to the kid.

'Palani'' replied the kid ogling at the heavenly beauty of the ten-rupee note offered to him.

Palani looked at each one of us with his interrogating eyes. Then his eyes spat on the scum that was us, who reveled in human misery, standing and smiling, dangling money in front of him.

If we deserved it for asking his presence at our midst, we were about to ask for more.

Tom got ready to start his charade.

He pulled out a five hundred rupee note and held it in front of Palani's eyes.

To my satisfaction, Palani's eyes did not register any surprise or greed; they remained circumspect at best.

'I will give you this money, a five-hundred rupee note if you get up and run to that tree all by yourself, without any help, on your two legs.' He threw the bait deftly.

I suspected he had been imitating his senior Palatt to the tee.

Palani did not move. He looked at the money without closing his eyes. It felt like eternity. Then his head sagged. His face registered tremendous pain, but not of the physical kind. Two teardrops silently embraced the 'four-wheeler' he was sitting on. His arms shivered slowly but uncontrollably. He opened his mouth to say something, avoiding eye contact with us, and then decided against it.

Tom did not act surprised. In the earlier case also, the victim did not break so fast.

We were not surprised either, as we knew Palani was not pretending to be a disabled person.

Tom pulled out another five hundred from his pocket.

'Here is another five hundred . . . Five hundred plus five hundred . . . full thousand rupees!' he held out the money as if it was worth much more than that.

'Just one dash to the tree, we will not ask you anything more, the money will be yours.'

Palani's shivering was intensified. Then he looked up. His eyes were moist. There was no venom in them anymore.

'Sir, I lost the ability to move my legs almost seven years back. It started as a mild fever. I was in a Government hospital for more than a month. When I was discharged from the hospital, my legs had turned into logs. The brick making factory where I had been working fired me. If my legs could hold me, if I could at least stand, I would not have sought alms and lead a miserable life,'' Palani said as more tears rolled down his cheeks.

'I did not ask you for an explanation. The money, thousand rupees, is yours if you run to that tree without any help. Otherwise, forget it' Tom was emphatic.

I felt bad for Palani. More than that, I felt bad about Tom. *People should not be so insensitive and cruel,* I felt.

'Sir, I cannot run. I cannot even get up. If I could, I would have gone, did some work, and earned a living. I would have sent my son to school. I . . . ' his voice trailed off getting lost in the breaking dam of frustration and anger.

He cried loudly, unlike a grown up man. His arms shivered even more.

Tom did not waver.

'Thousand Five hundred Rupees . . . final.' He added another five hundred and wagged them again.

'Daaaad . . . ' the kid wanted to say something.

Palani looked at his son. His wailing got louder. Then he stopped it as if someone switched off the speaker. His eyes fumed in anger and a fierce determination appeared to have engulfed him.

'I will try sir . . . I will . . . I need the money' shouted Palani in sheer desperation.

Then he looked at us with a faint hope that one of us would come forward and save him.

'Thousand Five hundred Rupees Palani,' Tom challenged him.

Palani lifted his body on his hands, making them bent a bit. One could make out he was in pain. His legs hung down from his waist still bent and crossed. Sweat broke on his forehead. His breathing got harder.

We watched without emotions. None of us had the courage to intervene, though each one of us wanted to.

He tried to open his legs but could not.

Tears ran down his cheeks. However, his face displayed no sadness. He was Angry; angry with the god who made him like this; angry with the man who was pushing him to do the impossible; angry at his desire for the big money offered; angry at the world, his misfortune, with us, with himself.

Then it happened. His hands gave way. He fell, head down first, from his seat to the ground with a '*thud*'.

We watched in horror.

I covered Anju's eyes. Like any good parent, I wanted her to grow up without seeing or understanding human miseries at close quarters.

Palani laid there motionless and defeated. He seemed all right though. Acceptance of defeat camouflaged the extreme pain he was feeling.

The Production Manager and I jumped to Palani's rescue. But he waived us off. He was defeated but not broken.

His son started wailing loudly.

Tom watched with equanimity. He was the only soul unmoved; at least I thought so.

Then he also showed signs of breaking down. As if pushed by an invisible force, he single handedly lifted Palani and put him back on his throne. Then he placed the three five hundred rupees notes firmly in Palani's hand.

'Let us go,' he said to no one in particular and started walking, without looking back.

As we walked out without a word, I handed Palani another five hundred from my pocket; the price of my guilt!

We climbed back in the SUV and continued on our course. Sandhya who was silent so far, vented her ire on Tom.

'Tom sir, what you did was unpardonable.'

'Sandhyaji, you don't get it,' Tom tried to defend.

'Come on . . .don't hang on to your stupid ego. Accept your mistake. Your game brought great sorrow to a poor human being, physical harm too,' she continued the tongue-lashing.

'*Etta,*[11]you should not be silent. If this film does not work out because of this, it is fine. What happened was inhuman and you have to drill it into Tom's head.' She decided to bring me into the confrontation.

'Tom, she is right.' I started in my diplomatic best.

Tom cut me short. 'No, you guys do not understand,' he said emphatically.

Sandhya turned her attention back to driving. Her face looked like an October evening sky ready to break into thunder, lightning, and showers.

'*Appa*[12], you almost lost thousand five hundred' shouted the relieved kid as the SUV raced ahead, tackling the curvy road ahead.

'You think so?' Palani asked.

'What if they did not give you the money and walked off? We would then be sitting here with the paltry ten rupees'

'What did you want me to do? Get up and run?' Palani asked extracting tobacco leftovers from his teeth.

'Yes, if that gave you more money than what you make in two weeks,' said the boy.

'You idiot, if they realized that my legs were fine, they would have taken that ten rupee also back, and may be they would have called the police too,' Palani said as he stretched his legs comfortably, allowing better blood flow to the feet.

[11] Etta - Typical way wives address their husbands in Kerala. Etta means 'big brother' in Malayalam.

[12] Appa - 'Father' in Tamil

'You could have taken the risk. It was thousand five hundred rupees.'

'Oh, Oh you and your thousand five hundred,' Palani feigned irritation.

Have you noticed the guy wearing white and white and the lady driver?'' Palani asked.

'Yes I did, what about them?'

'I realized they were potential suckers. Vulnerability was written all over them, especially the guy. I knew if I put in a tragic act, I could extract at least hundred rupees from him. . . . though I did not expect the full five hundred he threw in,' he chuckled as he extracted groundnuts from a small cover and threw them one by one into his mouth.

'*Appa*, that was great . '

'Son, I have seen all kind of people in the last forty years while begging on the road side. I can judge people easily, especially on their kindness levels and vulnerability. I am a great judge of people.'

The kid looked at him in awe.

'But you got the tough guy wrong, you did not expect him to give that thousand five hundred to you, did you?'

'No, I didn't. I still do not know why he paid that. Was my acting that convincing?' The question was more to himself than to his son, as he concentrated on the groundnuts.

****

Even the Assistants and the Production Manager sat with grumpy faces. Tom kept his silence.

Sandhya had been controlling her anger for some time. But she exploded like a pressure cooker after a few minutes, again.

'Tom Sir, I thought artists are sensitive individuals . . . you . . . you . . . you are heartless. Your thousand five hundred rupees do not compensate the ridicule you heaped on the poor guy. Thousand five hundred rupees do not wipe of your guilt, thousand five hundred rupees!' Sandhya was getting into form.

'Sandhyaji, please stop it,' Tom said; this time smiling.

'That money was not given to wash off my guilt. I did not feel bad even for a moment. In fact, I enjoyed the show,' he continued to smile.

'Tom, this is too much.' I intervened, this time seriously. It is not normal that I chide people and that too grown-ups.

But Tom did not allow me to complete.

'That was the advance money I paid to him for a role in our movie, a meaty role,' he said with a smirk.

'What?' All of us said together.

'His son sucks as an actor,' he continued.

'A great example on a how a scene can be unconvincing if your co-actor does not perform,' Tom said as if he is taking class for a bunch of acting students.

We sat dazed and beaten by the revelation.

Then an angelic voice flew in from behind.

'Dad, I knew that beggar uncle's legs were fine, his sandals were so worn out.'

All of us looked back at Anju in dismay.

This time, I realized even the great director registered a genuine surprise.

****

Shades of Love

'Sir, this is Mrs. Nalini Nathan,'' the receptionist of the facility ushered in the lady.

It was a sultry afternoon and I was in the process of losing a protracted struggle against a comfortable afternoon nap, when the sudden announcement woke me up. I could detect a devilish but well camouflaged smile in the receptionist's eyes in waking me up from a long awaited and satisfying siesta.

I studied the visitor from head to toe.

She was about 5 feet 4 inches tall and was elegantly dressed. Her dress and demeanor announced certain richness and a taste for fashion. She seemed to have had spent a lot of time in front of the mirror applying makeup which was evident from her apparently cosmetics free face.

'Come on in. Please have a seat.'' I invited her to my cabin and tried to make her comfortable.

The receptionist kept a folder on the table and walked back to the front desk, silently closing the door behind her.

'Relax,' I said to her in the best calming and soothing voice I could muster. This was the way I was expected to start my sessions.

I felt foolish as soon as I said it. The woman was much more relaxed than I was. She definitely looked quite in control too.

She does not look like the type who would visit a family counseling centre seeking help. Well then, I did not look like a counselor either! I thought.

'What would you like to have? Coffee, tea or a glass of fruit juice?'

Step two in our process book. Calm down the patient by offering something to drink. As a newcomer to the role, I did not want to skip any step, though this woman did not seem to have any need to calm down.

'A hot coffee would be perfect. You have a coffee vending machine. Isn't it? I remember seeing one at the reception.'

I pressed the intercom to inform the receptionist but she immediately dissuaded me.

'Coffee can wait; I generally have coffee after half past three.'

As a rookie, I thought I was losing control of the session. I tried to recall tips from the training sessions I had attended recently.

I needed to take charge.

'What should I call you, Mrs. Nathan or Nalini?' I asked fiddling the file in my hands.

The file contained her profile, and some health details based on all what she would have told the receptionist or filled up herself. In this case, I would not have been surprised, if Nalini herself filled all the forms.

Most of our guests needed help in filling forms, since their state of mind would not even allow them to hold a pen properly.

She looked very composed.

'Hmm Nalini,' she said softly.

'So Nalini it would be,' I said opening the file and looking at the information on the individual sitting in front of me.

Mrs. Nalini Nathan, to my surprise, turned out to be rather under-educated for the airs she carried. She had only finished her tenth class.

'Beauty and brains seldom go together; I found solace in the old saying.

'I thought all the counselors here were women,' she said as if to tease me.

'I guess, I as a man could help you see your husband's perspective,' I tried my hand at humor, which often fails me in the presence of attractive girls. I took my eyes off the file and closed it. There was nothing more of interest written in it.

'But if you are not comfortable, I would be happy to refer you to a lady counselor. She should be in by five,' I offered sincerely.

'No, you are fine,' she said with a tone of approval.

I was relieved. How would I be able to live with the shame of having lost the opportunity to help a damsel in distress, if she had opted for a woman counselor?

As a new entrant to the 'Family Counselor's Club', I had not had many opportunities to counsel grownups and more specifically women. My 'guests' - as we always called people, who sought our services, were students who were into either internet addiction or infatuations. I even had kids brought in for advice on higher education, but never an adult woman potentially with typical grown ups' complicated problems.

'How long, you had been counseling here?' she was not yet completely ready to accept me as a counselor.

'Three months, I joined recently.' I was fully on the defensive on this one.

'That is fine. What is your background? How long have you been married? Any kids?'

'Oh sure, yes, much married. I tried to lighten the conversation.

'I guess I have seen you somewhere. You are . . . you are an author, aren't you?' she asked.

'Yes, I am. You may have seen my photograph somewhere. I was interviewed by four or five journalists after my book was published. Have you, by any chance, read my book 'Curiosity Kills the KatHA'? There was a photograph of me on the back cover of the book', I tried to throw in some weight and tried to establish my credibility.

'No I do not read books. I have not heard of this book anyway. I think I have seen your interview in a newspaper and my friend who sent me here, said there was an author here. Anyway, that is not important.' She burst my bubble quite efficiently.

'So Mrs. Nathan, I mean Mrs. Nalini, what brings you here?' I did not like the way she was trifling my achievements as an author but decided to continue.

'Oh yes, I have a problem.' She produced a manila envelope from her designer bag and pushed it under my nose.

'Please have a look at this.'

I took the envelope from her but decided not to open it till I heard more.' What is this?'

She seemed to have read my thoughts.

'OK, then let me first tell you the whole story, before we come to this.' She changed her sitting position to make herself more comfortable, just enough to embark on a long story.

I put the envelope aside eager to hear the story before judging the relevance of the envelope in the big scheme of things.

'I had been married for almost ten years. My husband, you may have met him. On second thoughts, you are unlikely to have met him. I know people like you never visit government hospitals. I do not, for sure.'

'He is a doctor in a government hospital?' I tried to glean the information using the 'active listening' techniques I was taught.

'You are right. Dr. Kamal Nathan, my husband, is a surgeon at the government hospital in Jayanagar.'

'I see.'

My mind quickly tried to correlate the tenth standard pass on one side and a surgeon on the other side; 'educational disparity' among partners could be a ground for marital discord, if marital discord was her problem.

'My husband hails from a poor family in rural Karnataka. He was a good student from childhood and had managed admission on merit to Bangalore Medical School through sheer hard work.'

As an 'active listener', I was expected to prod the 'guest', but I did not think Mrs. Nalini Nathan needed any encouragement.

'He managed to win a scholarship and took a lot of educational loans to aid his journey at the medical school. However, when he passed out from the medical college, he realized that being a simple medical graduate would hardly help him in achieving the riches he had hoped for, once. So, he put his heart and soul into getting a postgraduate degree. That is where Nalini Gowda, daughter of the erstwhile real estate king Hanumanth Gowda, came handy. I was beautiful too,' she added .' The last sentence she added as an afterthought, but the casual glance in my direction was not. She was seeking my approval but I chose to ignore her last remark.

I, then realized that she was talking as if in a trance, without really looking at me.

'When did you get married?' I asked, though I knew she had answered this already.

'It is going to be ten years in January.' Her words were uttered in such a way that I immediately realized that ten years were a long time.

'Yours wasn't, as you indicated earlier, a love marriage.' Now that I suspected her case to be having some connection with her married life, I thought it sensible to get a better understanding of the marriage itself. *What better way than to state the known facts to extract the unknown ones?*

'Not at all,' she said as if she really regretted the fact.

'Oh, how did it happen?'

'It is not an interesting story. I was sitting at home after failing the pre-university college exams even after three attempts. I would have tried again, had it not been for an infatuation on my side.'

She raised her face and looked straight into my eyes and asked, 'Have you had love affairs during college days, Ashok?'

I did not know how that was relevant.

'I am afraid, I did not have,' I answered matter of fact. I was not here to give my life's secrets to every 'guest' who turns up for counseling.

'You are lucky. They just drain your energy and your partner selections often would be stupid, anyway.'

'I know,' I put on my 'mature' mask. I did not want her to realize that in my bid for suitable education and a decent job, I did not have time for such luxuries.

'I fell in love with our driver in the third year of my pre-university exam attempts. Probably he saw the same thing what the honorable doctor saw in me later'

'That was . . . ?'

'A short cut to money and a beautiful wife; should I say, a "trophy" wife.'

I could understand but did not want her to know.

'It did not take much for my father to get wind of the undesirable alliance. He naturally objected since the driver was poor. He was uneducated too. That intensified a search for a suitable match for me.'

'So Dr. Nathan's was an arranged alliance? But you said he too was poor?'

'He was . . . but he was well educated. My father was already facing a big trouble in business, was cheated by his partner. He had started trusting good education, which he never had, more than riches. Lack of education was his undoing. Considering his dwindling position in the market, he could not have found a great alliance for a lowly educated daughter of his, and there were two sisters after me also to be considered.'

She walked across the room, filled a glass with filtered water, and emptied it in a gulp.

'Doctor was looking for money to fund a post graduate seat in a private medical college and my dad was looking for an educated groom for his un-educated eldest daughter. Ours was thus a marriage of convenience.' She sighed recollecting the wedding.

'Our home those days was an example on how rich should live. My father used to wine and dine politicians and bureaucrats on a regular basis. My mother was a socialite of standing, and her kitty parties were praised by all who had the fortune to be invited. To say the least, we children were brought up in the midst of riches and pomp.'

'What about the doctor? How did he fit in?'

'He did not, never did.'

'Oh . . . uh,' I exclaimed.

'He was not just poor; his family was poverty itself. He was the only brother to three sisters. His father had escaped this hostile world, even before his only son could pass tenth. His mother worked as a part time tailor to bring him up. His sisters too had to join odd jobs just to survive. He was their only hope.'

'Where are they now?'

'They are in their village in North Karnataka. After our marriage, my father not only paid for Nathan's higher education but also helped him marry off his sisters and provide decent medical attention to his mother in her last days. My father was a good man at heart.'

'But you said your father's business was in doldrums.'

'Yes it was. But he held on to the secret till he got all of us married; all reasonably decent alliances. Then when his work was almost finished, he let us all know that his debts were well over the assets.'

'Where is your dad now?'

'He is no more. He too escaped, thanks to high cholesterol levels, his rich and sedentary life had gifted him and the heartbreaking experience of being declared bankrupt.' She stopped and sat with her head bowed without talking for a few minutes.

I thought it would be a good time to get her something to drink. I went out, stretched my arms and legs for a minute, picked up two coffees from the vending machine, and walked back to my cabin.

As I entered, Nalini was wiping teardrops from her sculpted face. She did that with a certain élan and made sure that her face remained transparently made up.

'Have some coffee,' I said.

'Thanks a lot. You chose the right time. I was a bit overwhelmed with emotions.' she said.

As she picked up her coffee, she re-started the narration.

'Where was I? . . . Hmmm, I was telling you about my father's sudden demise. My mother too died soon after. Anyway, I had moved to Jayanagar in Bangalore with Nathan by then. He had joined the government hospital here after his Masters degree. He is a good surgeon, you know?'

As she had said, I was not one who frequented government hospitals. Naturally, I had not heard of a certain Dr. Nathan, who was a good surgeon.

Even otherwise, if she does not know me as an author, how would I know her husband as a surgeon, anyway?

Nalini did not wait for any response from me to continue.

'Let me make the long story short. Nathan came home a Friday, six months back, very upset. As soon as he entered the house, he slumped down on the sofa.

I could sense the climax of her story just ahead. I sat upright in attention.

'I came running down from first floor as soon as I saw him. I could not believe my eyes. He was disheveled and had some minor cuts and bruises on his face and arms. His shirt was soiled. He looked as if he had fallen somewhere.

As I ran towards him asking hundred questions together, he shouted, *"stop."* He did not answer any of my queries; neither did he allow me to look at his bruises and take care of them.'

I tried to visualize that scene. Dutiful wife trying to help a distressed husband but not allowed to do so. Nalini, sitting in front of me, somehow did not fit the 'dutiful' wife image.

'After a couple of minutes of sitting like that, he got up and came towards me. I was still sanding, not knowing what to do.'

****

The day was the day of reckoning for Dr. Nathan. It started just like any other day for him. He got up in the early hours and prepared tea for himself and his wife, Nalini. She would normally get up a few minutes later. He, as usual, left home for hospital at 5:00 A.M. He had two surgeries scheduled for the day. He would have to eat breakfast at the hospital canteen.

Once the surgeries were over, he finished his lunch, again in the canteen, and reached his Out Patient room. The OP room, as it was often called, was nothing but a sixty square feet rat hole, which could barely hold a bed, two chairs, and a table. The nurse often found it difficult to find space in the room, while the doctor examined the patient.

Dr. Nathan had time before his OP session started. He stood near the window and looked at the imposing multinational private hospital, across the road. He sighed silently. If he had money to pursue a higher qualification abroad, he would have been working there. He would have had large spacious consulting room, and rich patients who loved expensive treatments for even simple illnesses. He would have had to meet only twenty or twenty-five patients every day, as against sixty to seventy- five he was forced to examine now. Above all, he would have had fat paychecks and expensive gifts from both patients and drug companies.

Everything else he could compromise on; But money, he needed lot of it.

His educational loans still had outstanding payments. While pursuing his post graduation, he had defaulted on two of these loans. It is true that his father-in-law had financed his post graduation. But by the time he bought an expensive flat, thanks to Nalini's tastes, his father- in-law had left the world.

Nalini's tastes, if only she did not have such expensive tastes, he thought.

Nalini had forced him to buy a large Toyota car for her. This was in addition to the small but useful Suzuki Alto he drove.

Cars meant loans and repayments.

Nalini's frequent kitty parties and shopping indulgences kept throwing up enormous bills. *I need to join a better paying hospital,* he thought, as usual.

In the early days of their marriage, especially after he came to know about his father-in-law's impending bankruptcy, he had tried reasoning with Nalini to live within his means. Frequent quarrels, over time, taught him not to foolishly try straightening the dog's tail. Instead, he chose the next best option.

Increase the means, his income as a doctor.

He started private practice at home. But when he was available for free consultation in the hospital, there weren't many interested in going to his house for the same services.

Then he started forcing his hospital patients to meet him at home, for the same services he was expected to give them free at the hospital. He demanded inpatients, at the hospital under his care, to pay him at home to get even minimal attention. He had also started demanding money from patients for surgeries he performed. He refused to perform critical surgeries on them if they refused to bribe him.

As Nalini embarked on more and more expensive pursuits, he became more and more ruthless about extorting money from his helpless patients. He had his loans to repay and as a doctor, he did deserve a decent life. Above all, as a son-in-law, he had to look after Nalini well, as the repayment of the great help, her father had provided him, and as a husband, he loved Nalini, despite her outlandish lifestyle.

To everyone, he was a heartless butcher interested only in money. But Dr. Nathan knew he was just debtor in many ways, trying to be a good husband, someone who could not face his own reflection in the mirror!

That fateful afternoon, while he was looking at his third patient at the OP, Dr. Nathan received a call from Casualty.

****

Ganesh was at the construction site, when he picked up the call from his neighbor Shankarappa.

'They sent Vinay back from school. He is complaining of severe stomach pain,' Shankarappa said.

'How bad is it? Where does he say the pain was?' Ganesh, unmoved, shouted in the mobile.

His wife Lalita, who was carrying a cement sack on her back looked in his direction and stopped.

'Don't really know. He is crying loudly.'

'He had a mild fever in the morning. Did not eat anything. The pain must be because of gas,' Ganesh said keeping bricks after bricks in to a jute sack he had kept on the floor.

'He claimed to have vomited in school. He said the pain was originally near his belly button; seems to have moved towards lower right, now.' Shankarappa seemed to be concerned.

'See he vomited. I say it could be gas only. The lazy bum does not go and play with other kids; that is why. Please give him a soda and he should be all right. Don't bother too much.' Ganesh tried to trivialize the problem.

'Ganesh, I have made him lie down by the side of the shop. You know I cannot take him to the hospital. I cannot close the shop now,' Shankarappa did not want to have the trouble on his hands.

With both the parents, working as construction laborers there was none in their hut to look after the six-year-old Vinay. Shankarappa was fine with the kid sitting in his shop till his parents came back from work but he did not want to be responsible for a wailing child.

'Shankarappa, that is fine. He will be alright in no time." Ganesh disconnected without waiting for a response and concentrated on his work.

'These bricks are of lousy quality,' he muttered, as one more brick broke as he lifted it.

Lalita smelt something wrong, but after seeing Ganesh's calm face, continued on her way carrying a heavy cement bag on her back.

Thirty minutes later, Ganesh's mobile rang again.

'Ganesh, Vinay is in a bad shape. He has vomited again. His tummy is bloated and hard. I do not feel good about it. Ayyanna who came by had a look at him and said he needs to be taken to the hospital.' Shankarappa seemed agitated.

Ganesh knew Ayyanna, the local old man, who knew a little of everything including medicine. But he did not believe that anything was wrong with Vinay. *Vinay always complains about some pain or other to avoid school, anyway,* he thought.

'Shankarappa,. Please do not bother. Vinay does all kinds of drama to avoid going to school. You go about your work.' He disconnected the phone again without waiting to hear more from Shankarappa.

Good that Lalita was nowhere near. Otherwise, she would have created a scene, Ganesh thought.

The third time the phone rang; Ganesh suspected that something was wrong. This time Shankarappa sounded panicked.

'Ganesh, I am taking him to the Government hospital. His condition is worse now. We are already in an auto rickshaw. Ayyanna is also with us.'

'What! Shankarappa, is it that bad . . . ?' Ganesh exclaimed.

'You come directly to the hospital; we are taking him to the casualty section. We will be there in ten minutes,' Shankarappa shouted and disconnected.

Ganesh was stunned. He sat with his palms holding his head. Vinay was their only son and he could not imagine that something could be seriously wrong with him which warranted a hospital visit. Shankarappa would not have taken the pain unless it was an emergency.

He saw Lalita racing toward him.

'What is wrong?'' she asked.

From his expressions and body language, she had figured out that something was wrong, very wrong.

'Nothing,' Ganesh tried to act calm.

'Nothing?'

'Uh, Shankarappa called. Vinay came back from school complaining of stomachache. I asked Shankarappa to take him to a doctor.'

'Shankarappa is taking him to a doctor?' Lalita instantly knew things were bad. Ganesh would never ask such a help unless Vinay was in bad shape.

'Where is he taking him?'

'To the Government hospital, I am going there."

The Government Hospital! Things must be really bad. Otherwise, Shankarappa would have gone only to the local clinic, she thought.

'What is wrong with my Vinay?' Lalita started crying. As her crying grew louder, other workers crowded around her.

'Do not make a scene Lalita,' Ganesh shouted.

'I am coming with you,' she said without stopping her crying.

'OK, I will get some money from the supervisor and come.' Ganesh walked off to the site office.

With the thousand rupees wage advance he could extract from the site office, Ganesh and Lalita rushed off to the Government Hospital.

At the casualty ward, they met gloomy faced Shankarappa and Ayyanna.

Vinay was lying on a makeshift stretcher holding his tummy tight. He was obviously in severe pain. As soon as Lalita saw Vinay, the intensity of her crying increased. Vinay, however, was too weak to cry loudly.

'Please observe silence,' a stern looking nurse shouted.

Shankarappa took Ganesh aside and whispered, 'It does not look good. The doctor on duty had one look at him and said it was an appendix related issue. He needs to undergo an emergency surgery, it seems. Otherwise, his life would be in danger. '

Ganesh felt the whole world coming down around him. *His frail six year old undergoing an operation!* He could not digest that.

'I have called the surgeon from OP. He will come any time. Only one person can be with the patient.' One of the nurses said as she pushed all of them out. Ganesh stayed back near Vinay. He could hear Lalita sobbing outside.

He counted the money in his pocket. Only thousand and three hundred rupees!

Would that be sufficient for the operation? he wondered.

He walked out leaving Vinay alone and asked, 'Shankarappa, do you have any money on you?'

Shankarappa examined his pocket and handed over six hundred rupees to him. Ayyanna produced two hundred more.

Two thousand and one hundred rupees that should be sufficient. This is a government hospital and everything should be free. He had to spend only if some medicines were not in stock, he felt comfortable.

Dr. Nathan walked in casually but briskly. He was pulled out just after he had finished examining his third patient in the OP.

'Where is the patient?' he asked.

Doctor on duty came running in. As they examined Vinay together, Ganesh could hear many medical terms being thrown back and forth.

He only could understand that something was very wrong with his child and something had to be done immediately.

'Who is the bystander[13]?' Doctor Nathan asked matter of fact.

'Doctor, please save my boy,'' Ganesh pleaded moving closer to the doctor.

---

[13] The person who stays with/accompanies the patient in the ward.

Nathan studied the man standing in front of him. One look at him and he could make out that this man was a laborer. His heart sank.

When the call from casualty came with the prospect of a surgery, he was elated. These patients often needed immediate surgeries. In such circumstances, he could demand and get far more money from the patients than in normal cases.

He needed money badly.

Payments for Nalini's new car had been stuck for the last few months. House and education loan payments too had been affected, thanks to the down payment on the car.

I need to somehow bleed this person for money. I need to get at least twenty thousand, he calculated.

'See, the problem is with the boy's appendix. Appendix is a small finger-like organ that is attached to the large intestine on the lower right side of the abdomen. That is why the pain in that area. His appendix is infected and inflamed.' Dr. Nathan tried to explain the problem in a simple and clear manner.

I need to sound knowledgeable, confident, caring, and capable of solving the problem before I demand money. They should feel, I am 'God' who could save their child. Then they would cough up the money somehow. I need to act like the only one capable of saving him, Dr. Nathan thought.

God, I hate to act so heartless.

'We need to remove the infected Appendix. If the appendix is not removed, it can burst and spread bacteria. That will be very serious. The boy may not survive, if we do not operate on him right away.' He stopped and looked at Ganesh.

Ganesh stood dazed. He did not understand most of what was said. But he realized that his son is facing a life or death situation and only an operation could save him. Only *this* doctor could save him. He looked at the 'duty doctor'. He was affirming everything, the surgeon had been saying.

He felt confident about the surgeon.

'Doctor, please save him, how much ever it costs,' Ganesh begged without thinking.

'You do one thing. You come to my consulting room in half an hour,' Doctor Nathan said, and prescribed medicines to reduce the pain and gave the prescription to the nurse on duty.

He walked back to the OP room as briskly as he came.

One has to look serious about one's profession, he thought as he walked watching the flurry of activities his prescription had kicked off.

Ganesh and Lalita entered Dr. Nathan's consulting room ten minutes early. They could not hold themselves to wait for the full thirty minutes the doctor had suggested.

'Come in,' Dr. Nathan cordially welcomed them and asked them to sit.

'Vinay's mother,' Ganesh introduced Lalita as a courtesy.

'Doctor, please save my Vinoo,' Lalita, who had already been updated about Vinay's illness and about the surgery suggested by the doctor, pleaded and started sobbing.

Ganesh sat silently with bated breath waiting for the doctor to talk.

Doctor signaled the nurse to leave the room.

'So, what should we do? Shall we go ahead with the surgery?' Dr. Nathan asked in an upbeat voice.

'Yes Doctor,' both said simultaneously.

'OK, good decision.' Doctor waited as if to measure both of them before discussing the next issue.

Then, as if by compulsion, he said 'I am afraid, it would cost you some money'

Ganesh was all attention.

'Not much, a few thousand rupees only,' he said trivializing the amount and waited to see their reaction.

'You know this is a major operation and we cannot do without it. I will do everything to save your boy.'

'How much would it be doctor' asked the helpless father?.

'It would be about twenty thousand. Medicines and other things, I will take from the pharmacy here. We won't charge you anything more.'' He noticed the shock registered on Ganesh's face.

'Normally, I would have charged thirty for this, since you seem to be hard pressed, I have decided on twenty.'

'Doctor, we do not have that kind of money. I have only two thousand one hundred with me,' Ganesh emptied his pockets on the table.

'Don't say like that,' Lalita chided her husband. Then she turned to the doctor.

'We will give everything to save Vinay,' she hastily removed her bangles and earrings. Doctor noticed that she did not have a necklace of any sort.

'Doctor, please take all these and save my boy,' she started crying.

Dr. Nathan looked at the light silver ornaments on his table.

These would not fetch even two thousand, he thought.

'Take all these. I will give you half an hour and I do not care where you get the money from. If you want to save the boy, bring full twenty thousand,' Dr. Nathan's voice was no longer cordial.

Ganesh cringed as if a snake bit him.

'And remember, an hour later, any money you bring would be of no use. I may not be able to do anything. Go fast and find the money,' he said with finality.

'Nurse, next patient.' He shouted at the nurse outside gesturing them to vacate his room.

Then his heart wept, with no visible tears on his face.

****

Thirty-five minutes later, Ganesh was back at Dr. Nathan's consulting room. This time Shankarappa had taken Lalita's place. Lalita who had been beating her chest uncontrollably and wailing loudly, was in a bad shape to be brought to the doctor's room.

This time, they did not wait to be ushered in.

As soon as they came in, the doctor sent out the patient who was in his room and the nurse outside.

'So you brought the money?' he asked, trying to see where the money was hidden.

Ganesh produced the Rs. Four thousand and change, nearly double the amount he had offered to the doctor earlier, collected by pawning his wristwatch and Lalita's ornaments in a nearby shop.

Dr. Nathan quickly estimated that it was less than even five thousand, and refused to touch the soiled notes.

'What is this?' he asked. He was annoyed and surprised.

'We could put together only this much', Ganesh said apologetically.

'I see that . . . you can take your son somewhere else,' Dr. Nathan was cut and dry.

'Doctor, please be kind, we will pay the rest of the money within a week.' Ganesh could not control tears.

'Don't bother, I do not have anything to do in this case, you can take your boy somewhere else, as I said.'

'Doctor, this hospital is supposed to be free, why should we pay money?' Shankarappa intervened.

'Because I had spent lakhs of rupees to get this degree and I need a way to repay my loans,' Dr. Nathan said sarcastically. 'And by the way, who are you to ask me? Go . . . go and complain to the police if you want. Your boy would be dead by then anyway.'

The first slap came when the doctor least expected it!

He should have noticed Ganesh's features changing, while he was challenging Shankarappa. It was the inevitable aggression of a person, who had everything to lose, but nothing to lose by being aggressive.

Then the blows came like rains. Hands that carried bricks felt like hammers.

Shankarappa bolted the room from inside.

Ganesh lifted the doctor by the collar and shouted, 'You will do the surgery free, doctor. If you do not, I will wring your neck myself. Make sure that nothing happens to my boy during or after the surgery.

Then he dropped doctor back on to his seat.

Ganesh knew his son would be saved. He could read that much in the doctor's eyes, it was not fear alone!

****

Dr. Nathan met Ganesh and Shankarappa that day once again. As soon as he returned to his consulting room after the emergency surgery, the duo barged in unannounced.

'Doctor, thanks a lot for saving my son's life,' Ganesh said sincerely.

The doctor did not want to look at their face. He wanted the kid to be healthy again and discharged ASAP from the hospital. He just wanted the ordeal to end somehow.

He was not used to being slapped around by people and he was not ready for another session.

'Doctor, please do not be angry with us for what we had done. If your son is on the deathbed and you run out of all options, you would have also done the same,' Ganesh tried to explain.

Doctor was in no mood to listen. His body was paining. More than that, his mind was on fire.

From the moment, the surgery was over, he was thinking about himself; about his journey from a poor boy to a government doctor; about what had become of him. He tried to analyze how he became like this or who had changed him.

As he escaped the two and drove through the narrow lanes to reach home, only one thought, a question nagged his mind.

Who should he blame? The blame for getting him beaten black and blue by two laborers!

He knew the answer too well, only he was responsible for his behavior.

But there was another person to share the blame. Someone who continuously pushed him to greed and debt by lavish lifestyle. Someone whom he owed his masters degree and his family's well-being; someone who was stubborn in the continuous effort for high society acceptance; someone whom he loved more than anyone else despite all flaws, his wife Nalini.

She was to be blamed in equal measure!

****

That fateful evening, as soon as he entered his home, he loosened his necktie and slumped on the sofa.

Nalini came running down from first floor. She was as usual, clad in a costly sari, and looked ready to go for a party.

For some reason, that day, she did not look quite beautiful. She looked plain and homely.

Seeing him with swollen lips and random bruises, she stopped for a moment. Then she raced towards him.

'Stop,' he shouted. 'What happened? Look at you, did you fall somewhere?' she asked a hundred questions in one shot. Nathan could feel the genuine concern in her voice.

'Leave me alone for some time,' he said loudly in a much harsher voice than usual.

She could make out that he was agitated.

She stopped herself in her tracks. She did not know what to do.

She could have stood there for couple of minutes. He sat at the sofa slouched and uncomfortable.

Then he got up and walked towards her.

The first slap fell on her, when she had least expected it!

It was the first in their married life.

He continued hitting her, though she blocked most of them with her hands.

Her face burnt and her mind caught fire.

'Stop it,' she first shouted and then pleaded. Tears rolled down her cheeks.

'Why are you doing this to me?'

'I am sharing what I got today, my partner,' Nathan said sarcastically, stopping the physical violence and turning away from her.

'What?' she shouted as she collected herself. 'Have you gone mad?'

'No I have not. This is the 'returns' I got for all the greed and sin I had invested in as a doctor,' he said pointing to bruises on his face and arm.

'I just shared half of it with you as an equal partner,' he said in a raised voice.

Nalini by now had regained herself.

'I do not want any such share.' Her voice had a sharp edge.

'I demand money, undeserved money. I extort my patients, to feed your life style and desires. I share the money I make with you. So I want you to share my wounds too.' He did not give up.

'I do not want to share your wounds,' she said looking directly in his eyes.

'I have to share it.'

'Not with me.'

'Aren't you ready to share my sins?' Dr. Nathan asked as if the question would decide their future.

****

'After beating me up he asked me *'aren't you ready to share my sins,'* Nalini said gulping water down quickly.

I looked at the woman sitting in front of me. Her long story has taken enough twists and turns to take me to an unknown territory.

'So the Doctor had a *Valmiki*[14] moment?' I asked.

'What . . . oh yes, a *Valmiki* moment it was.'

'What was your answer?' I asked though I could guess what it was.

'Obviously, I said a firm *no*. I did not want to share anyone's sins. It was his duty to take good care of me. After all what he is today was made possible by my father's money.'

I could not find holes in that argument.

'Moreover, everyone takes bribe nowadays to do things. It is no great sin,' she added.

'Then . . .?' I did not want to be stuck on ethical question like that.

'Then he stormed out of the house and has not returned till today.'

'Six months!'

'Yes six months, he has started living with another woman, an old flame of his from school' she said matter of fact.

'And the envelope contains his divorce notice,' she added.

I looked at the envelop as if it represented the biggest injustice to my guest. 'I am here to seek your organization's help in getting us back together,' she finished her story.

'Do you love him still even after he slapped you and left for another lady?' I asked.

---

[14] Valmiki Moment - Valmiki, a sage, is the Author of Indian epic 'Ramayana'. The legend has it that he was initially a dreaded dacoit. One day Sage Narada happened to pass by his territory. When he ran into Valmiki, he ordered the Sage to give everything he owned or face death. Narada asked Valmiki if his family was part of the sin that he was committing. When Valmiki asked his parents if they were with him on the sin that he was doing, they replied that it was his job to take care of them, and that he was only responsible for his own sins. His wife also said the same thing. Enlightened, Valmiki gave up his sinful ways and converted himself to sage.

'Sir, it is not love. It is something else. I am sure I cannot survive with anyone else. He was the best I could hope for.'

She was at least frank about her reasons, I thought.

'What about him?'

'I do not know. I guess he would be equally happy with that woman.'

I still had one doubt nagging me.

'Did that lady agree to share his *sins*?'

She looked at me for a few seconds as if to decide on how to answer my question.

'When I received the divorce notice, I called him. I asked the same question.'

'What did he say?'

'He said she too refused to share his *sins!*'

'What? then how?' She stopped my question halfway.

'But he said she had agreed to share his *poverty*'

I did not know what hit me!

'Are you also ready to do that now?' I recovered and asked a question, pretty much knowing the answer.

'No., I want you to get us back together somehow,' she said.

'If you are not ready to come down in your stand, where is the chance of a compromise?' I asked.

'Who said I am not ready to? I am ready to come down. You can confirm to him that I would readily share his *sins in the future.*'

She once again surprised me.

It took me another hour to complete her case file. Finally, I made her to verify the copious notes I had made, for factual accuracy and got her out of my room, after fixing another appointment for the following week.

Once the privacy of my room was regained, I dialed my wife's number.

'Hey, I have a question for you' I said.

'Shoot' she replied in her normal jovial self.

'Are you ready to share my *sins* or *poverty?*' I asked seriously.

'I don't know what you are talking about' she responded continuing to play the *Veena*.[15]

I repeated my question.

'I don't know what this is all about. You do not have any work at the counseling centre?'

'No you need to answer this question . . . now'' I insisted.

'OK, then tell me, what was the question?'

I repeated the question, 'Are you ready to share my *sins* or *poverty?*'

'Whatever it is, I do not want to share you, everything else is shareable, I guess,' she disconnected the phone.

Knowingly or unknowingly, meaning it or without meaning it, I realized, she had just given me the answer I wanted.

****

---

[15] Veena - A musical instrument

Three murders

'I will wait here ma'am. Take your time,' I said as the lone passenger got down from my auto rickshaw[16].

'Can I leave all these here?' she asked pointing to two-three cotton bags she had kept on the floor of my auto rickshaw. They were packed. I did not venture to ask her what was inside.

At the outset, judging by the bags, I did not think the contents were anything precious.

Even if I go for a quick coffee leaving them unattended, no one is likely to steal them, I thought. Nevertheless, I need to make it doubly sure.

'Hope there is nothing costly in there? Something, I would want to steal?' I said in jest but requiring an answer.

'Definitely not, I made all those myself, and I do not seem to have made anything worthwhile in my life anyway,' she said broodingly.

Loaded statement! I thought.

I got a bit curious. Whatever is inside is made by her! What could that be?

My customer, a demure old woman, walked towards the temple slowly. She must have been about seventy or seventy-five. She

---

[16] Auto rickshaw - A three wheeled passenger vehicle common in India.

was dressed in a red silk sari but did not have any gold ornament on her, which typically characterized rich women visiting big temples for morning prayers. But I could see aristocracy written all over her.

I was obviously not in a hurry, neither was she.

'Son, do not drive too fast. I have all the time in the world,' she had said as soon as she got into my auto-rickshaw.

After I drop a few kids in their school, I do not normally get *savaaris*[17] till at least nine thirty. So, I preferred to hang around the Palace Road auto stand till some office-going gentleman engages me for trips to MG road or Indira Nagar. This gave me ample time to finish my home packed breakfast, sitting below the sprawling Banyan tree and read the day's top news stories in the local newspaper.

Today was not any different. Except that, the petite old woman walked to my auto as soon as I had reached the stand and asked an unusual question.

'Are you ready for a long *savaari*, son?'

'How far ma'am? If it is outside the city, you need to give me return charges as well. It will then be double the meter charge.' I made my policy clear.

'No it would be just inside the city. But I need to go to quite a few places. All seven to eight kilometers apart. You would just have to wait at each place for me to come back,' she explained.

'In that case you need to pay only the meter charges plus the waiting charges if any,' I was relieved. We auto drivers always liked short trips which allowed us to be within our own territory. That often helps us to meet old acquaintances or complete odd jobs without dedicating any extra time.

---

[17] Savaari - a hired trip in an auto rickshaw

She looked at me for a moment, trying to judge my trustworthiness. This was not the first time, when someone looked at me in surprise when I told him or her that they had to pay me only the meter charges. I knew Bangalore auto drivers often demanded 'over the meter' charges even for small trips.

The only thing I had inherited from my mother other than poverty was the worthless pride in my integrity and principles. *Possessions, which hardly helped me to make a decent living!*

But my new passenger seemed to be unaware of her luck in meeting a principled auto driver.

'Ma'am, it would be great if you could give five minutes for me to finish my breakfast,' I requested.

She thought for a moment.

'Why can't we do this? You take me to the Anjaneya Swami temple at Guttahalli first. When I go for *darshan*[18], you can finish your breakfast. That way we would reach before the temple closes," she made an alternative suggestion.

That is how I turned up at the temple in time for *darshan*, which I seldom did. My God could be pleased only with good deeds and not frequent visits and adulations!

As she got down and walked towards the temple, I opened my breakfast pack. My wife Janani always packed breakfast for me. That helped us to save money. Lunch was a different thing. I had to have my lunch wherever my auto rickshaw took me. It was difficult to keep packed lunch without being spoilt, in an auto rickshaw, especially in hot weather.

Breakfast was the same every day. *Raagi Mudde* - Raagi Balls. It never tasted great, but it has been the traditional breakfast for me as long as I could remember, because it was the cheapest, my

---

[18] Darshan - Visiting God and praying.

family could afford. Over a period, I had developed a tolerance at first and later a soft liking for it and the affordability question continues to be valid even today.

My mother had taught me to crave for only things I could afford.

After finishing breakfast, I took a little time cleaning the windshield of the auto rickshaw. It gets dirty quite fast in the dry weather.

My passenger climbed down the steps slowly holding on to the side rails carefully ensuring that she does not slip accidentally and walked towards the auto.

At this age, what a love for life! What care! I thought.

'Here, take a bit' she offered me the *Prasad*[19].

I took a bit from her palms and consumed it with respect.

She rearranged her bags on the auto rickshaw floor and climbed in.

'Did you have your breakfast?' she asked. A mother's concern was evident in her tone.

I answered in the affirmative by nodding.

'I didn't get your name, son,' she said a bit tentatively.

'Lokesh, Ma'am, Lokesh Shetty'

'Great, Lokesh. Do you know the Sapna Book House near 15th cross? I need to go to a house near that' she said.

I started the auto and got back on the road in no time.

Within a few minutes, we arrived at one of those traffic jams, which permeates every nook, and corner of the city.

'So you brought breakfast?' she asked, I guess, just to make conversation.

---

[19] Prasad - a material substance of food that is a religious offering in Hinduism, which is consumed by worshippers

'Yes ma'am, I do that every day.'

'Raagi, wasn't it? I can smell it' she said.

I nodded.

'Your wife prepared it?'

'Yes, ma'am.'

'She has to be a very good cook, if you carry the food she cooks, everyday to work.' 'Hmmmmm, she does a decent job I guess and preparation of *Raagi Mudde* does not demand one to be a great cook anyway.' I tried to accept the accolade gracefully.

'Who all are there at your home?' she asked in a more serious tone.

It was not usual for my passengers to treat us drivers as fellow human beings, let alone ask questions about our family. For most, we were just extensions of the vehicle, who cannot hear or understand conversations or actions.

Here is someone asking about my family and me. Even if it is for just passing time, it is refreshing, I thought

'Ma'am, my wife and my only son.'

'Oh you have a son?' she asked. Her voice conveyed a mix of emotions, which I could not understand.

'Yes , seven years. He goes to the government school, Nearby.'

'Educate him well so he could develop wings and fly away, and reach dizzy heights,' she said quite poetically.

I visualized my son completing his education and joining a high paying job, in my mind's eye though I did not like the 'fly away' part in her statement. Why 'away'? Why not be 'with us'?

May be I would retire then and spend a lot of good time with my wife, I thought.

We, my wife, and I rarely spent time together from the day we got married. I work all seven days and spend most of my time with my Auto rickshaw. She worked in a textile factory nearby, and reached home early enough in the evening to complete household chores and prepare dinner. Our son is in the school till late afternoon, and waits outside his mother's' work place till she finishes her work every day. We definitely miss some family time.

I realized I had broken the conversation, having fallen into my own wishful thinking.

'Ma'am, what about your breakfast? Are you planning to eat at the house we would be going to? Or do you want to stop near a *Darshini*[20]? 'I asked.

'Hmmm yes, I need to eat something. If you are ready to share, we can eat some sweets together.'

She opened one of her cotton bags and took some traditional sweet items from it.

'I made all those,' she had said, I remembered.

So, it was only food, only some sweets. She had made some sweets probably to distribute to various relatives as we went from house to house, I realized.

'These are yummy, just the way my mother used to make them,' I lied purposefully.

The sweets were good.

The lie was about my mother. She never made sweets as far as I could remember. If she could make enough money to give her

---

[20] Small vegetarian restaurants in Bangalore, where people stand and eat traditional food.

four children, Raagi balls three times a day, she would have died a much happier woman. She was seldom Happy.

'Oh I see, your mother is still alive?'

'No, she died long back. She died of lung cancer. She used to work at a construction site. I guess the cement dust did not agree with her.'

'Oh, I am sorry, and your father?'

'I did not have much attachment to him. He was a drunkard. My mother was his second wife and he married again three months after I was born. If you do not plan to take care of your wife or bring up your children, once could marry any number of times,' I said sarcastically.

'No son, don't be angry. Everyone would have sound reasons for every one of their actions. It is just that the others do not see it. Your father might have had one as well.'

'Oh, he did, not one but many, I am sure,' I muttered.

She did not speak for some time.

I tried without success to imagine what could have been my father's reasons.

Silence crept in between us.

'Take a left here and stop near the second house,' she instructed.

'That grey bungalow?'

'Yes, that is my brother's house. You can stop here.'

She slowly climbed down from the auto rickshaw and picked up one of the cotton bags.

'I do not think I would take more than thirty minutes. I am going there, after seven long years. I don't know how they would welcome me. You wait here only.' Saying this, she walked towards the house with uncertain steps.

I found it surprising that she had not been to her brother's house for seven years, especially since, they were only three - four kilometers apart.

May be some distant cousin, not own brother, I thought.

I waited patiently. She came back in less than thirty minutes.

She was still clutching the cotton bag in her hand and it was not empty!

As she climbed in, I could see traces of tears on her face. She seemed to have wiped it off before getting out of the house.

'Your cousin brother's house?' I asked not wanting to keep her in that mood too long.

'No my own brother . . . my only brother.'

'Oh, uh'.

'My sister in law died seven years back. That was when I came to this house last.'

'Who is living here now?'

'His son and family. His wife had died before him. He had two children, the other one, an engineer, is in America. This one is an accountant,' she volunteered information without really being asked for it.

'How come you never dropped in here?'

'That is a long story. You would get bored with it.'

I started the rickshaw and moved out of the bi-lane, and then realized I did not know the next destination.

'Ma'am, where should I take you next?' I asked.

'Oh, I forgot, let us got to RMV second Stage. Keep on the 80 feet road. You will see a brown building near an apartment complex. Drop me there.'

I picked up speed after we reached the main road, but was soon back to crawling as we were caught in bumper-to-bumper traffic.

'You were telling about your brother.' A little story is always welcome, in our otherwise boring job.

'The story is more about me and not so much about my brother,' she said as a preamble.

I could not care less.

'I was born in Bangalore.. Those days, it was not a crowded city like this. Even places like Malleswaram and Basavangudi were more or less considered outskirts.' She started her story in the classical story telling tone.

I have heard such statements from many old people. It was fashionable for everyone to talk about the good old Bangalore in the good old days and complain about everything new.

If nobody liked progress, how did it come about? I always wanted to, but never bothered to, ask anyone who made those statements. I did not believe in arguments, anyway . . . but I truly believed that progress was desirable and nostalgia was only a defense mechanism to avoid accepting the improvements the passage of time brought.

'My father was in government service. We were from a well to do family with roots in Western Karnataka. My parents had only two children - my brother and myself. Though our upbringing was quite traditional - We were *Brahmins*, you know - being an educated man, my father encouraged us to study. In my case, when all my friends got married at eleven or twelve, I was allowed to go for higher studies and I even attend a graduate course.'

She took another sweet from one of her bags and offered me. This time, I courteously declined.

'Those days, we used to visit Bowring Institute with our parents. Bowring Institute, you know, is an elite social club in the middle of the city on St. Marks Road. Being a member was a matter of pride. So we two used to wear that on our sleeves.'

Members of the Bowring Institute! I have seen the institution many times during my trips to MG Road and knew that it was meant only for the rich and the aristocratic. I could see that my passenger still displayed discernible aristocracy, though she no longer seemed to be taking it that seriously.

'Bowring was full of military officers and planters, men, especially from Kerala, who had huge coffee plantations in parts of Karnataka and spent most of their time and money in Bangalore. It was in one of our trips to the club that I met Peter Pulikkunnel, son of a wealthy planter from Kerala.'

I started liking her story. Rich Brahmin girl and equally rich Christian boy set in mid twentieth century, enough for sparks.

'Remember, when I met Peter, I was not a very young girl by our standards. I was twenty and was doing my final year BA[21]. He was twenty-seven then and had completed his studies to join a brewery in Bangalore.'

I could see a bit of shyness spreading on her face as she relived those moments.

'Let me guess,' both of you fell in love,' I tried to move the story at a quicker pace.

'Not so fast son,' she laughed. But the sadness in her eyes remained.

---

[21] Bachelor of Arts - An under Graduate course.

'But you are right about that. It was a handsome boy meeting a beautiful fair girl of compatible age. When that happens, caste, religion, social status, everything is forgotten. You only see each other and then try to see the rest of the world through the other's eyes. Have you had the opportunity to imbibe that feeling?'

I hate it when people talk about love and romance. My childhood memories had scarred me enough to prevent me from succumbing to such finer feelings in life and the poverty-ridden life demanded an extremely focused life — earn the day's meal.

But I hazarded an answer considering the fondness and respect I had already developed for my passenger.

'I had been brought up with the memories of my father, mostly based on the stories I had heard from neighbors and village folks. My mom never ever said anything bad about him. I never saw him, as he had left the village long before I could roam around and look for him. Seeing my mother laboring so hard, after she was abandoned by my father, my adolescence never brought me dreams of romance and marriage. So, to answer you, I never could partake in such enjoyable fantasies.'

I knew I was a bit caustic in my remarks.

She did not seem to notice the edge in my words. Even if she had noticed, she let it pass gracefully.

'So how did you get married? Arranged one?' she asked.

I sincerely hoped she would get back to her story rather than dig up my background.

'When my mother finally fell sick with no one to take care, I had no option but to get a girl home. Hiring a girl to nurse my mother was costlier than marrying one. So I married the first one who accepted to look after my mother.'

'So you married only to get someone to nurse your ailing mother? That is interesting ... Did she finally?' she asked as if that was abnormal.

'Of course, she did.'

'So there was no love!'

'Once she came in and started taking care of my mother and me, we did fall in love, though that was an after effect,' I said.

'Let your life abound with that love, son,' she said with her eyes closed in a prayer.

'Anyway, coming back to my story, where was I?' She decided to continue.

'You were talking about your romantic escapades with a Christian man.'

'Oh yes, Peter was a great person and mine was an impressionable age. So we fell in love, a love affair, which lasted thirteen years.'

Her eyes had gone moist. I pretended as if I had not noticed.

It did not make sense. How could they continue their romance for thirteen years? The girl would have been much beyond her prime then.

'When we decided to marry each other, the rest of the world objected. My parents and his parents forgot religion, social status and everything else and joined hands to oppose our marriage. We have never seen such camaraderie between bride and groom's families. They joined hands only to oppose our marriage.'

'I can understand your parents opposing, why should his parents?''

'Son, in India, though we talk about abolition of caste hierarchies, in our mind we strictly hold on to that very notion. Look at yourself. When you asked that question about a *Brahmin*, you implied that *Brahmins* being considered the highest caste, no one, no other caste or religion would object to a relationship with *a Brahmin girl.'*

'That is the reality ma'am.'

You may be right in most cases but Peter's family was different. His family strongly believed that they were the descendants of the Christians who arrived in India from Syria along with Thomas of Cana and hence superior to most other Christians in India, who were essentially converts. For them, any wedding in the family had to be with someone from a similar family and even a *Brahmin* girl hardly matched their expectations.' In effect, everyone was against your marriage,' I said.

'Yes, not just against. My parents permanently banished me from my house. I was never allowed to meet and talk to my father till he died. In fact, whenever I tried, he refused to meet me; he insisted that he never had such a daughter. My mother was only used to obeying my father and she refused to meet me as well.'

'That sounds bad.'

'It was worse. My father died within two years of my marriage. He is supposed to have told many that he would rather die than see a successor born in his family with Christian blood. He succeeded in his wish. He died of heart attack caused by high blood pressure. My son was born three months after his death. It was the first murder I had committed,' she said with a resignation in her voice.

'No, you cannot call it murder. He died probably because of his flawed beliefs,' I tried to console her.

'You may be right, but what is murder anyway? It is nothing but causing some one's death through one's actions and that exactly was what I had done. I had killed my father by marrying a non-Brahmin. I cannot absolve myself of that crime.'

If you define murder like that, everyone you meet on the road is guilty of genocide, I thought.

I did not want to argue the point too far. Not because I agreed, I wanted her to get back to the story.

'Then there was my mother. If she had obeyed my father because of her respect and fear for him, while he was alive, she obeyed him more, after his death as her penance for giving birth to me, the girl who killed her father. My mother refused even to look at my first born, my only child. She did not speak to me even at the time of Peter's death. She lived long but lived miserably, I guess.'

'What about your brother? Did he also cut-off all connections with you?'

'My brother was not a fool and was not hung up on religion, class, and similar notions, I am sure. But he also ignored me, initially to support his father as a dutiful son.'

'So after your father's demise, he would have re-established contacts, probably without your mother knowing,' I asked.

Traffic had started moving slowly. I had not noticed that we were less than two kilometers from her next destination.

'He did not. By then he would have realized the economic benefits of not doing so. He had started usurping everything my father owned and our disconnect had been quite handy.'

'Haven't you tried to contact him?'

'I did; many times, but he refused to entertain me. I was not welcome at his home. Whenever I had been to his home, he refused to meet me. After a number of such humiliations, I stopped trying to patch up with him.'

'That is too bad; people do such things for money?'

'People do, most people do anything for money, and each one has a different threshold though.'

'You mean how far they would go?'

'No, on how much money one needs, to commit the most heinous deeds.'

'So you have not met him after your marriage?'

'Oh, no, I did several times, but as strangers.'

'How did your husband react to all these?'

'Peter? ... He could not care less. He did not want any money from my family. He was making enough and spending enough; we never faced a financial crisis, at least till he died'

'How was Peter as a person?' I had started asking questions as if I was investigating a murder case.

'He was a nice husband, a caring father and above all a great human being.'

'I guess he also died soon, isn't it? You said your mother did not turn up even for his funeral. How did he die?' I was now crossing the decency limits, probing her life's secrets, but I could not help it.

'He was a gentle and loving soul I told you, he had been working at a brewery. We were a happy family. In those days, we used to go to the vineyards in different parts of Karnataka with our child - John - for holidays. Peter, for one particular trip, borrowed an old Ambassador car from a close friend. He was a good but slow driver. He was very cautious on the road and often drove singing old Hindi songs.'

I could visualize the romantic youngster on an outing with his loving family in some picturesque locale, in a borrowed Ambassador.

'The trip was particularly exceptional that day. We enjoyed a lot. On our way back, we were passing through a small village when we saw a small boy getting beaten black and blue by some laborers. True to his character, Peter wanted to speed off. He never believed in involving himself in any trouble, any time. But I asked him to stop. I had this habit for poking my nose into injustices around me and responding to them. He gave in finally, and stopped near the crowd. I got out of the car.'

'You got out!' I expected Peter to do that, however indifferent he was.

'Yes Peter and John sat in the car as I got down.'

'Then?' Curiosity was killing me.

'As soon as I got down, they stopped beating the boy. The boy was lying on the floor writhing in pain. *'Don't you guys have any sense, beating a small boy like this? All of you together? What has he done?'* I shouted at the top of my voice. My arrival in the car, demeanor, and the courage with which I faced them had stunned them for a few minutes.'

'That is true, the villagers often show respect to the city bred, especially women; sometimes unduly,' I added.

'Ma'am, you don't have any business here. Please go away. We will handle these ourselves, one of them shouted back at me. Then, I realized that they were all drunk. My sense of justice did not allow me to leave the boy at the mercy of those hoodlums. I pushed one of them and grabbed the boy. Before they could realize what was happening, I pushed him into the car and jumped in. Since Peter had been running the engine, we gained some ground before they decided to follow us.'

'They followed you?'

'Initially they did not comprehend what I had done. A few of the mischief-makers chased the car on foot. Peter tried to speed away. They started throwing stones and whatever they found handy. Two of them got on to a two-wheeler and started following the car. As I said, Peter was not the best of drivers when one had to move fast. The fear of chasing hoodlums, made him press the accelerate hard, and the car suddenly was out of control. When I woke up next, I saw Peter covered head to toe in white cloth, ready to be buried. God had left me and John unharmed, to face the cruel world. That was my second murder,' she fell into silence.

This time I did not want to question her definition of 'murder.' However, I started feeling that she probably had a point in accepting the blame. I also did not want her to continue in that mood too long. I wanted to ask her something so that she could go ahead with her story.

'What happened to the boy, they were beating?' I asked as if that was the most important aspect of the incident.

'Oh, ah, he escaped with minor bruises and ran away before anybody could catch him. Apparently, the kid had broken open the local temple *hundi*[22] and tried to take away all money. They had caught him red handed,' she said as if the boy deserved to be beaten for what he had done.

I did not agree with that either. I believed it was humans who needed the money and Gods did not have any reason to hoard them. My God definitely did not need money to survive and He would never be angry with someone who takes His money without asking.

'John was only ten when Peter departed leaving me alone to take care of him. I took up the challenge, having been left without

---

[22] Hundi - Place where people put money as offerings in the temple.

options. Then I realized that we had been spending everything we earned and we practically had no savings. I was not left with much to take care of John. That is when I started working as a tutor for a few students at home.'

'Was that enough?'

'It was not at all enough. I was forced to visit my brother again after a long time and demand at least a portion of my share of dad's property and he once again, refused to meet me.'

'How was his wife and children?'

'His children were too young to make a difference those days. But his wife had been always nice, warm, and welcoming as long as her husband did not notice her being a good host to me. She, in his presence, was forced to act cold.'

'At least, that would have been quite heartening to you.'

'It was, but there are no certainties in life. When I ran out of all options, I filed a suit against my brother demanding my share of the property. The litigation dragged on for years . . . five years, but finally I won the case.'

'Aha, at last a solution to your financial troubles,' I asked partially relieved that my passenger may not be too poor to pay me as her story was making me believe. Anyway, she, as I had suspected, looked pretty well to do.

'What solution? For five years, I did any job, including menial jobs at rich houses to bring up my son and pursue my case. But you are right, the court order did save me from financial hardships. The share I received was good enough to make me 'rich' by even Bangalore standards.'

'Then?'

'Then I committed my third murder.'

She said without any emotions but my heart missed a beat.

'What!'

'Yes, this time it was my only brother. He could not digest the fact that I had won the case. It was not so much about losing the money or the property. It was more about being caught in the act, the act of commandeering someone else's possessions. So, he decided to take a revenge, in his own way. He ended his life with an overdose of sleeping pills. Thus, he succeeded in depriving me of my sound sleep for many years. I was responsible for his death too. My third murder, so to say,' as she shed tears silently.

'Ma'am, where do I need to stop?' I asked when I realized that we were nearing her destination.

'Third house on the left ... that brown building. Otherwise, you do one thing, you stop here, I will walk from here,' she said and wiped her tears with one of the ends of her sari. The silk sari failed to absorb much.

She saw me watching through the rear view mirror and smiled faintly.

'Let me wait for two minutes and complete my story as I do not want them to know that I have been crying.'

I wondered how she would complete her story. What else was left in it for her to *complete*?

'After my brother left the world, my sister-in-law developed a deep hatred for me. After all, as far as she was concerned, I was responsible for making her a widow!'

'As you had been saying, you were the murderer,' I said in jest.

'Yes, I do believe it. It must have been my *Karma* to be a murderer. Anyway, I met her one last time seven years back, as a corpse. It was a natural death and that one definitely could not be attributed to me! I did go to the house, where we had been earlier today, to have that last meeting and to my surprise, they did not chase me away. However, I was told in no uncertain terms that I would not be welcome in their house anymore. My nephew had grown and had learnt to be like his father.'

'What happened during today's visit?'

'What is there to happen? My nephew refused to meet me and he got his little nine-year-old daughter to tell me to leave the place. The sweets I had made with these hands . . . they were snatched from the young kid's hands and I was ordered to leave the house and not to come back again. They seemed to have ensured that the kids learnt about their rich bad grand aunt who had killed their grandfather. I was reminded of my crimes, not by words, much worse, by actions. That too by those small kids, unknowing as they were' Her crying was more intense now.

I did not know how to pacify her. I kept quite.

She tried wiping her face again. This time she produced a handkerchief from her bag and it was much more effective than her sari.

'Let me meet these relatives and come back. You be around. This, at best, will take less than an hour, 'she said.

As she got down, I could not help asking her one question.

'Ma'am, you knew how badly you were going to be treated, when you went to your brother's house today. Why did you go there?'

She looked at me and smiled after a lot of effort.

'I will let you know, let me finish the work at hand first.'

Saying this, she walked slowly towards the brown building.

A small cloth bag in her hand, full of sweets, danced to some unheard melody.

I got down from the auto and tried to stretch my arms and legs a bit. I realized that my lethargy did not arise from a long driving session but from a draining story.

As I walked around aimlessly, my eyes fell on the nameplate screwed on one of the pillars of the compound wall of the brown house.

It said Jose Pulikkunnel, advocate and notary. I deduced that he could be related to my customer's in-laws in some way.

I also realized I had forgotten to ask her about her relations with her in-laws throughout her narration. Then, I was not used to prying.

I waited.

She did not take the expected time here also. However, when she returned, her hand was empty and the sweets had disappeared.

For no reason, I felt happy for her.

As soon as she occupied her seat, she opened the remaining cloth bag and offered me some fried food item. This time, it was something similar to a *Bajji*[23] and was not very sweet. Slowly, savoring the taste, I started the engine.

'Do you know William's Town near Bore Bank road?' she asked

'I think so. Where in William's town do you want to go?'

'There is a Mother Mary's Church near the Corporation School there.'

'I know it. It is near the junction of Pottery Lane and Bore Bank Road.'

---

[23] Bajji - A fried snack in south India.

'You are right. Let us go there next.'

I accelerated towards the new destination.

'You went to meet your in-laws this time?' Knowing well that poking into my customer's affairs was not expected of me, I asked.

'Oh, you saw the nameplate?

'Hmmm,' I said sheepishly. She has seen through me.

'Jose, mentioned on the sign plate, is Peter's nephew. However, he does not live here anymore. He has gone back to Kerala a few years back and has settled down comfortably near some river bank.'

'Who lives here?'

'Peter's only sister's elder son, Jose's elder brother. He is a computer engineer. Those guys do not keep name plates like lawyers and doctors,' she said with a bit of sarcasm.

'I know. They work in big companies, drawing fat salaries. They have no need to interact with common people,' I added. I somehow hated the software engineers who polluted the Bangalore lanes with their fancy cars and fancier languages.

'Tom is a big guy in some big company. I have not met him for a long time.'

'You did not tell me how your relationship shaped up with your in-laws after your uh . . . complicated marriage,' I tried prodding.

'Ah I missed it. I told you, they too fought tooth and nail to stop our wedding. Peter's parents never pardoned him for the big mistake. His father formally removed him from his will thus removing any chance of us inheriting anything.'

'So both of you were effectively disowned'

'There were differences too. Since there was no potential of fight for share from his side, his only sister - Liz - pardoned him after the parents' death. But by the time the siblings got back into speaking terms, we were already over ten years into our marriage.'

'You must have got some support from Liz after Peter's death, didn't you?'

'I wish I did', she said with a sigh.

'Why? What happened?'

'There was another reason why Liz pardoned and moved closer to Peter. She was facing some major problems in married life and needed someone to advise and support her; someone responsible, someone she could trust. Marital troubles, which forced her finally to file for a divorce and custody fight. Who better than her own brother, could help her?'

'So that is another tragic story?'

'Not a long one though. Liz's husband was a blue blood Syrian Catholic accepted by her family. His pedigree allowed them to condone his laziness, lack of education and alcoholism. In addition, his family was not a rich one; but his ancestors were part of the Syrian visitors.' Her tone was biting.

'So they got what they deserved?'

'I cannot comment on that. But Liz realized that her husband's boozing parties were slowly wiping out her father's plantations and at that rate, she would have to go begging on street by the time her kids went to college. Peter, the trusted advisor, suggested divorce from her loafer husband. There was no other solution anyway.'

'But you said there was a child custody issue as well?'

'Yes, there was. Her husband thought he was entitled to half of her plantations, and to force that, he demanded the custody of their children.'

'How was it settled?'

'Peter, always a staunch believer of peace, worked out a solution, acceptable to both sides. Liz got to keep her two children and sixty percent of the plantations and her husband got the remaining forty percent. The divorce was through mutual consent.'

'At least things ended in a happy note.'

'Well almost, as I said, Liz's husband was an alcoholic. Once he got a good amount of money in hand for unbridled spending from the divorce formula, he decided to indulge in intense "spiritual" pursuits. His liver did not quite cooperate, and the soul left the body after a few weeks of painful existence in a private hospital. Then the pangs of guilt caught up with Liz. She started blaming herself for that death.'

'All you people seem to accept guilt quite easily,' I said.

'You are probably right. Liz not only accepted the guilt, but shared it too. Peter, according to her, became the perpetrator and accessory to the crime. Rest of her life, she lived like a recluse, spending her time and money on prayers and meditation and nurturing an intense hatred to Peter; after all, he was the one who suggested the divorce. I guess one hates the most, the ones who helped the most.'

I was not in a mood to debate philosophical points.

'So, you lost the only support or at least the only connection you had with all relatives on either side?'

'Yes and our accident happened in less than two years after Liz's divorce.'

'Who did you meet today?' I wanted to jump ahead on the story.

'Liz's elder son Tom was not at home. He was out of the country. I met his wife; daughters have already gone to school. She was nice to me and accepted the sweets gracefully.'

'So you should be happy.'

'I should be, but when you meet your nephew's wife, after a long time, you expect some warm welcome. I met an indifferent woman who would have preferred my not turning up. Anyway, I am happy that I came and met at least her and I sincerely hope she wouldn't throw the sweets in the dust bin.'

By then, I noticed, we had turned beyond the corporation school road and Mother Mary's church was right in front. As I stopped the rickshaw, she jumped out and walked briskly to the church like a much younger person. She seemed to know in advance that she would be welcome there.

'I will be back in two minutes,' she shouted on her way.

'Are you going in to atone for your three murders?' I shouted after her in jest.

I could see her entering the church and talking to a nun. The nun went inside and brought an older colleague. They talked for a few seconds and my passenger handed her a small packet.

Before I could guess what was happening, she was back in the auto.

'Where to . . . next?' I asked.

She started from where she had left, answering my question.

'This visit has nothing to do with my murders. They have pained me all along and will continue to pain me as long as I live. I came here for a different purpose. There is an orphanage attached to the church. Peter used to donate money to support three children here, until he died. I defaulted in the first five years after his death due to my financial difficulties. But once I received my share of my father's assets, I had re-started the practice. I just paid for the next five years in advance. I do not want to default again, at least for the next five years.'

'That was nice of you,' I commented. I could not think of anything else to tell, though I would have loved to continue the conversation.

'You did not tell me where I need to take you next.'

Then she noticed that I had not even started the rickshaw.

'Oh I forgot, not very far. You know Bangalore East Railway station, don't you?'

'Oh yes, that is just over a kilometer only...'

'That is right. Somewhere near that comes the East Park. You can drop me there and proceed.'

'So that is it? You do not want me to take you back to where I had picked you up?' I had assumed that I was to take her back.

'No, my trip ends there. You will get another customer from the Railway station.'

I was speeding past the East Railway station area, when she suddenly asked me to stop.

I stopped without knowing the reason.

She jumped out and walked to a roadside toy vendor to pick up a nice looking car. I guessed such a battery operated remote controlled car would cost not less than three hundred rupees. She paid the money, got the toy packed in an old newspaper and came back to the vehicle.

As soon as she sat down, she gave the package to me.

'Hey, this is for your son. Tell him an old lady gifted it to him for having a nice mother.'

I was surprised.

'But ma'am, this costs a lot of money!'

'It didn't. Moreover, it is my prerogative to decide my gift.'

I did not argue and took her to the East Park without hurrying.

Why did she say 'nice mother' and not 'nice father?' I wondered.

For some reason, both of us were lost in thoughts during the rest of the journey, though the traffic stretched it to over five minutes.

I stopped the rickshaw, and got out at the park.

She still sat inside as if she was thinking about something.

I waited patiently.

'Would you mind passing on these sweets to your family? I can't take them with me,' she said with some apprehension.

Those were meant for someone else and she is now giving it to me because they had refused to accept it, I thought.

In normal circumstances, my pride would not have allowed me to accept it. But we had developed some connection in the last few hours that I felt duty bound to accept it.

I did.

She got down, opened her purse, and pulled out a thousand rupees note.

I looked at the meter and calculated.

'Ma'am it is only two hundred and seventeen. I do not have change,' I said as I wiped the windshield with a dirty napkin.

'Me too,' she opened her purse fully and turned it upside down. There was no money left!

'OK, let me run and get change from some shop' I said pointing to a row of shops little away on the opposite side of the road.

'Do not bother,' she said.

'What!'

'You were such a nice companion. Take it as a present from your mother.' She put the money in my hand, left me with my mouth agape, and walked with steady steps towards the park.

I just stood watching her.

As she disappeared behind the trees, I decided to stop for the day. *I had already made much more than what I would normally make in two days.*

As I sat in my auto deciding on what to buy for my wife as a special gift, a nagging doubt seeped into my mind.

What if there is no one in the house, when the old woman turns up? She does not have any money with her. How will she get back home without money?

I decided go in search of her and give her at least the change for hundred odd rupees I had in my pocket.

I entered the park and looked around. I could not find her.

I saw a peanut vendor lazily frying peanuts on a hot stove in one corner of the park.

'Hey, did you see an old lady going out of the park?' I asked.

But a passing train just a few hundred feet from the park, beyond the trees, completely drowned my question.

I waited for the din of train to finish and then repeated my question.

'A lady in a red sari?' he asked.

'Yes.'

'She went that way,' he pointed towards the railway tracks.

I was stunned!

'You know her? Mental case? There are no houses beyond the track on that side,' he continued.

I did not say anything. My mind was racing through every sentence she had said, trying to connect the dots, avoiding the obvious conclusion.

'Hey, she might have gone there to commit suicide. Has she disappeared without paying the auto charges?' He pronounced suicide as if it was such a common thing.

'Shut up, don't say such things,' I admonished him as I ran towards the track.

My heart was beating fast, almost uncontrollably.

There, at a distance, I saw the frail figure covered in red near the tracks. From the distance, it looked like large red bundle, a lifeless one.

I ran towards the bundle with all my might. My arms and legs started shivering. I prayed for a miracle.

Then, I saw her more clearly, sitting crouched near the rail tracks, crying profusely.

I thanked God.

I did not realize how fast I reached her; the time had probably stopped for me.

I touched her back in an effort to comfort her. Time elapsed without both of us noticing.

We did not say a word.

Then I made her get up and walk with me, holding her close to my body, to the waiting auto.

She sat like an obedient child in the auto rickshaw.

'Where to Ma'am?' I asked without knowing really, why I had asked that question. It sounded stupid from the time I uttered the first syllable.

'Back to where, we started, Palace road. I will tell you the house when we reach there,' she said without any emotion in her voice.

Her coldness sent another shiver down my spine.

I started the auto and drove past the East railway station.

I could see the railway employees walking around, oblivious of their escaping another suicide on the tracks. I had heard of engine drivers scarred mentally for life after witnessing people throwing themselves in front of their engines.

Someone got lucky today!

I wanted to talk to her, more importantly, I wanted her to talk...

'Ma'am, I understand that your relatives, on either side, are not in good terms with you. But does that demand such an extreme step?' I asked.

She did not say anything.

'I suspect, no I know, you had planned everything, before you got into my auto. First, you went to the temple, then to each relative's house and met each one of him or her one last time. Then you made good the payments, you had missed, at the orphanage. Finally, you gave whatever money was left, to me. The last act in the script was to end your life on those railway tracks. Everything makes sense now.' Anger was evident in my voice.

What right I had to be angry? Who was she to me? What Injustice had she done to me?

She still kept quiet. Her eyes told me I was right.

'But one question Ma'am, what about your son? How would he take it? How can you do this to him? Or is he also dead?' I guess the sense of injustice was making my words harsher.

This time she spoke.

'No,. John is very much alive. He is married and has two children. I stay with them.'

'Then what is your problem?'

'John works in an Indian multinational; in the software industry. His wife also works in another software company'

'They do not take care of you well?'

'You know, your priorities always change after you get married. That is probably what happened with John. I guess it should be that way. The most important person in a husband's life should be his wife and the next has to be the children. Initially, things were fine. They needed someone to take care of the kids. I fit the bill perfectly. That helped my daughter- in-law to continue to pursue her career. When both the kids started going to school, things started to change.'

'How?'

'Then this old lady started becoming a nuisance in their life. When they wanted to go on holidays, they had to arrange someone to come and sleep at home to ensure my well-being. Generally, the old people are always trouble for the young ones, whether you like it or not.'

'That is there everywhere. Nothing new about it.'

'Yes it is; I agree. But fate gave an additional twist in my case. I fell ill last year. It started as reduced appetite. Frequent visits to the doctor had been already getting on everyone's nerves, when the doctor announced that my kidneys were slowly failing. I am on my way to becoming a dialysis patient soon.'

'I can't believe it!'

'You would expect everyone to be more sympathetic. But realities are different. You cannot blame anyone. Last year John had an opportunity to go to the United States for work and settle there. He wanted to go. He was even planning to take me along. That was when they found that my kidney was failing. They could not take me and there was no other place for me to go. I think my daughter-in-law started hating me since then. John would not have been happy either; one does not get such breaks often, you know.'

I wanted to ask something but decided not to.

'First it started with a coldness in relationship. The grownups started acting as if I do not exist. Then conversations between them started giving me implicit hints about their unhappiness about me and my deteriorating medical conditions. I started to realize that I had finished my purpose on earth and soon realized I was a liability.'

'But what precipitated your decision now.'

'Yesterday, my elder granddaughter asked me innocently - grandma, when will you die?' I thought it was an innocuous question. 'As soon as God calls me dear,' I told her. 'Grandma, please ask him to call you fast. Otherwise, dad will not take us to America this time also, the five year old told without understanding what she had asking from me.'

'That was childish. Why did you take it seriously?'

'Yes that was childish. But I noticed by accident that both parents who had overheard her question had not tried to correct her! They didn't say it explicitly but they didn't regret her saying it!'

'Hmmm.'

'Then I thought a lot about my life. I realized that if I had thought from their point of view, I would have reached the same conclusion. The old woman has overstayed her welcome in this world. Now she was standing in the way of her own son's progress, his family's future. Which mother would want to do that? That is why I made the plan, prepared some sweets for all those who had special places in my life — at least whoever had been left of them.'

We had pretty much reached the destination.

'Hey, you take this left turn and right ahead stop near that gate. That is my son's house'

'And you found my auto to execute the devious plan,' I said sarcastically while bringing the vehicle to a stop as she had instructed. I could not think of anything else to say.

'All the best son, we might meet again,' she said walking towards the gate.

'Same to you Ma'am. One last question though. You went to commit suicide, why did you decide against it. You were on time and the train did pass near you... but you never jumped. Why? Got scared?' I asked.

She stopped abruptly on her tracks. Then she laughed, — this time quite a hearty laugh.

'No son, not at all, I was not scared...but when I thought about my son one last time, when I saw his face in my mind one last time, I realized I did not want him to feel bad even for second . . . feel bad about causing my death . . . just the way I regret my three murders. I did not want him to live with any regrets. No mother would. We all love our children soooo much.' She then squatted on the ground and cried.

'No Mother would.' Her voice echoed in my ears.

Then I saw a young man coming out of the gate shouting. He pulled her inside, without even looking me.

'Mom, Where were you. We were looking for you all over the place. If something had happened to you, what would people say,' he continued.

I did not hear the rest.

Here is a son who is more worried about 'what people would say' than "what if something had happened to his mother.' That too, a mother who just saved him from the guilt of a murder! I tried to figure it out.

Like a zombie, I got into my auto and waited, just in case she wanted a trip back . . . back to the railway tracks!

I realized, I would have happily driven her to the destination. She deserved an escape; her son did not.

However, I knew no mother would take that trip.

****